DON'T SAY A WORD

Also by Debby Meltzer Quick

McKinney Class of 1986
May I Have Your Attention Please
I Just Can't Say I Love You
Absolutely and Totally Smitten

DON'T SAY A WORD

ANOMALY: BOOK 1

Debby Meltzer Quick

To anyone who has ever felt unheard and misunderstood.

Kaya: Freshman Year

SHE HAD DREAMED OF IT for years, and now it had finally come true: She had made the cheerleading team. The road had been long, filled with dancing lessons and gymnastic classes, but it was worth it. She loved the work. But it didn't feel like work. It had been harder on her parents than on her. They were the ones who'd had to get her to her lessons and then bring her home after. They had to endure all the hours she practiced at home, sometimes blasting the music so loud the chandelier in the dining room shook. Bouncing up and down on her bedroom floor with each jump didn't help. With the first crack in the ceiling, her parents demanded that she move her practices to the basement or outside. They didn't want their house to collapse with them all inside.

Now she was on the cheerleading team—as a freshman. Only three freshmen had made it through tryouts. She had gotten the top spot. Being the most petite of the bunch, she would also get the top spot on the pyramid.

It was about more than just being short, though. In order to be on top, she also had to have skills. She not only had to climb up over five other girls, but when she got there, she would need to maintain her balance, and stand up on the backs of two of her teammates. It was challenging work, and a bit scary. But Kaya was so excited, she didn't care. She would be cheering for the varsity basketball team. Nothing could be better.

It almost made up for the other thing. Almost. Kaya was still trying to figure out what was going on at home.

Just months earlier, during the summer, her father had made an announcement: He was leaving. He had to go. He couldn't say why, but he could say that it wasn't anything that Kaya, her brother Graham, or their mother had done. He loved them all, and that hadn't changed. He just had to go. No one even feigned to understand what he was telling them, but it didn't matter. He packed a single suitcase, put it in the cab, kissed them all on the cheek, and was gone. And he hadn't come back.

Kaya was still waiting for him to come back. He hadn't. He hadn't even been in touch. She could tell her mother was waiting, too. She often sat on the couch, silently, her hands folded on her lap, her expression blank. Kaya and Graham left her alone in these moments. They had no idea what to say .

But cheering helped. Being cheerful was Kaya's thing. She had always been the one to encourage others. It made sense that she would do it officially. And today was the first day of practice after school. She was excited. She had no idea what to expect.

Practice started with introductions and an ice-breaking exercise. Miss Green, the coach, made them share their names, their favorite movie, and the names and favorite movies of all the team members that had gone before them. Then, when the circle was complete, the first person who went would need to recall everyone's answers. It was chaotic but fun. Everyone concentrated hard so they wouldn't forget names. Kaya learned the names of the other two freshmen on the team, Bailey and Jill. Bailey seemed like a happy, easygoing girl, but Jill looked like she'd rather be anywhere else. She was probably just nervous about the first day.

They spent the first hour working on basic cheers and moves. The next day they would do more extensive routines, and they would have a week to practice them before the first basketball game. The first pyramid would be on day two. Kaya couldn't wait. Nervous energy was building up in her stomach. She wanted to do it just right, to show everyone how ready she was, how much she deserved to be there—as much as everyone else.

That night, she told her mother and Graham all about practice. "The girls seem really nice," she said. "I like them all so far. Everyone seems really giddy."

Graham smiled. "You'll fit in so well," he teased.

Kaya grinned. "I know, right? And tomorrow, we do the pyramid. I feel like I've been getting ready for this moment all my life!"

Mrs. Reed smiled. Her smile was warm, but since her husband had left, there was little happiness behind it. "I'm happy for you, Kaya," she said. "I can't wait to see you cheer." She turned to Graham. "Would you be able to pick Kaya up after practice tomorrow, honey? I have so much to catch up on with work. It would really help me out."

Kaya could see pain on Graham's face when he looked at their mother. "Of course," he said. "If it helps, I can do that from now on. I don't have anything to do after school. I can go to the library after last period and do my homework."

Mrs. Reed nodded. "Thank you so much, Graham." She looked back and forth between her children. "The two of you are so wonderful. I'm so lucky to have you both."

Kaya felt a pang in her stomach. She felt bad for her mother, but more than anything else, she missed her father. At the same time, she was angry at him. It was confusing. Sometimes, she had to block out those thoughts so they didn't overwhelm her. Since her father left, she was overwhelmed very easily. But cheerleading was her salvation.

The next day, Kaya arrived at cheerleading practice ready to go. She wore her new uniform and had her pom-poms in hand. The team did their warmups, and then worked on their simple routines. Miss Green taught them a new routine, and they worked on the steps. Then came the moment Kaya had been waiting for: the pyramid. Miss Green gave instructions for the older girls to help the younger ones get into position. It was safer for the younger girls to climb on top of each other, so the older ones were assisting and spotting them. Kaya was finally ready for the top. A senior girl gave her a boost, and she climbed onto the backs of Jill and a sophomore named Penny. She got herself in position and balanced.

"Are you ready, Kaya?" Miss Green called out. Kaya nodded. "Okay. Sarah, stay close. When you're ready, Kaya, stand slowly, your knees bent. That's it. Good. Keep going. Tuck your chin. Arms out. Great! Nice!"

"I wish you would fall on your head and die so I could be on the top," Jill said.

Kaya looked down quickly. "What?"

No one responded. She figured she must have misheard something, so she reached for the pom-poms that Sarah was holding out for her. She slowly held them up over her head.

"Maybe not die," Jill said, "but at least get hurt. But I could never push you. I don't have the nerve."

"Kaya, focus!" Miss Green yelled out to her. "Your mind is drifting. You need to keep your head in the game! Why don't you get back down on your knees for now and work on your balance? Are the rest of you holding up okay?"

All of the girls indicated that they were doing fine.

When the girls got down from the pyramid, Kaya approached Jill. "Why did you say that?" she asked.

Jill looked at her, puzzled. "Say what?"

"Those things you said when we were on the pyramid."

Jill's eyes narrowed. "I have no idea what you're talking about," she said. "I didn't say a word when we were on the pyramid."

"Okay, girls," Miss Green called out. "Circle on the floor, please."

Kaya looked at Jill once more, but then Jill turned around and headed over to sit in the circle. Kaya watched her go. She thought for a moment. Could it have been someone else talking? Was it the acoustics in the gym? Maybe she'd heard wrong. She shrugged. She must have been mistaken. No one wanted her to fall off the pyramid. She was just overwhelmed with everything that was going on with her father, not to mention the excitement of being on top of the pyramid.

But it had seemed so real. . . .

No, it had been real. She knew it. Her imagination wasn't *that* vivid.

She would have to see what Graham thought about it.

Chapter 1

GRAHAM REMEMBERED THE FIRST TIME it had happened, at least to his knowledge. He was picking up his sister at cheerleading practice. It was her first year on the team, and she was fourteen. She looked pretty in her uniform, the sweater vest and the little pleated skirt. She had her hair up in a high ponytail, and she bounced toward him with her pom-poms. "That girl over there," she said by way of greeting, "the one with blond hair? She wants me to die."

Graham looked at Kaya sideways. "I know cheerleaders can be fierce," he said, "but I don't think she wants to actually kill you."

Kaya dropped her pom-poms on the floor, then bent down to tie her shoe. She shook her head. "No, she really wants to kill me."

"How do you know that?" Graham asked, humoring her. He thought maybe there would be an interesting punchline coming.

Kaya got on her feet and shrugged. "She said so." She started toward the bleachers to grab her jacket and backpack.

Graham rushed after her. "So you're saying that this teenage girl, this tiny little blond-haired, blue-eyed cheerleader in small-town America, just said she wanted to kill you out of the blue? Why would she want to kill you?"

"Well, she didn't actually say she wanted to kill me," Kaya said, slipping her arms into her jacket. "She just said that she hoped I'd fall off the top of the pyramid and die." She zipped her jacket.

Graham shook his head. "This doesn't make any sense. Did you piss her off or something?"

"Not that I can think of," Kaya said, looking up at him. "I don't know. Let's just go, okay?"

They started to walk toward the door. "So she just said this, right in the middle of the pyramid? That seems weird. And you don't even seem all that upset about it."

Kaya jerked her head back and furrowed her brow. "She's not gonna actually do anything," she said.   "And I don't know if anyone else heard. Although it was kind of loud."

"How do you know she's not gonna try something next time?" Graham asked. He was already planning on having to tell his mother about the homicidal cheerleader at Wisteria High.

"She said she didn't have the guts to do it herself. She said it would be nice if I fell, but she'd never actually push me or make me fall. Then she just stopped talking for the rest of the time. It was weird."

"Wait," Graham said, stopping in his tracks. "She said she wanted you to fall off the pyramid so you would hit your head and die, and then she said she wasn't going to kill you, but she liked thinking about it, and then she started talking about her homework . . . all while six girls were in a pyramid formation, and you don't know if anyone else heard her? Does she talk like this all the time?"

Kaya looked up in thought. "No. Well, I really don't know her yet, so I don't know.   I guess it was kind of weird that she started saying all that stuff in the middle of practice, and no one else said anything. Maybe there's something wrong with her, you know, mentally."

Graham started walking again. "Maybe," he said. "I'll tell you what. Keep an eye on her, okay? Let me know if she says anything else like that about you. If she does, we need to tell Mom. We can't have people threatening you. Maybe she was just joking around."

"I don't know," Kaya said, shrugging her backpack up higher on her back. "Jill doesn't seem like the kind of person that jokes around a lot. She's really serious. She's really competitive. She didn't like that I got chosen before her on the team. She thought she was better than me. She told the coach that she thought she should be the one on top of the pyramid. She's really not as good as she thinks she is. And she does think she's pretty special." She opened the passenger side door of Graham's car. "Maybe that's why she wants me to die. So she could be the one on top after I'm dead. Huh. I guess that makes sense."

Baffled, Graham got in the car and started the engine. Kaya was not the type of kid to tell stories. She never hid her thoughts, or her feelings. She was smart, cute, and everyone he knew liked her. Would another girl her own age really say something like that? And if she did, why didn't the coach say something? Graham had played JV baseball, and he knew the coach would never have let anyone get away with saying things like that during practice. Plus, he simply didn't know anyone who would say things like that. Maybe Jill really did have something wrong with her. He shrugged it off.

The next day, Kaya joined him after practice. She scrunched up her nose before she spoke. "Now Jill says she wants to put laxative in my milk at lunch so I have to miss practice to go to the bathroom with diarrhea, and she can take my place," she said. "And this time, she really means it. I'm not gonna drink any milk on practice days anymore. I'll only drink from the water fountain."

Graham stared at her. "You've got to be kidding me. When did she say this?"

"We were doing a cheer, and we were all spread out, holding hands. Jill just said it. She said, 'I'm gonna get you, Kaya. This time I can do it.'"

"Did you say anything back to her?" Graham was watching Jill walk across the gym with two other girls, chatting and smiling. How could everyone just act like none of this stuff was happening?

Kaya shook her head. "No, it was too loud with everyone cheering," she said. "And I had to concentrate on my cheer."

"Did she say anything else to you during practice?'

Kaya shook her head again. "No, she only seems to talk to me when she's close by. I wasn't close to her after that."

"We need to say something to Mom."

Kaya turned quickly to look at him. "No, Graham, please, don't say anything, okay? I don't want Mom coming into school and making a scene. It would be embarrassing. I want to be able to handle this myself. I'm in high school now. Besides, Jill's not gonna try to hurt me badly. I mean, she told me what she's gonna do. Like I said, I just won't drink any milk. I really can handle it."

"Why would Jill tell you what she's gonna do, Ky?" Graham asked. "I mean, now you know, and you won't drink the milk. It's more like she's trying to scare you."

"But I'm not scared. I'm not afraid of Jill. I'm not afraid of anyone."

He gave her credit. She didn't look scared.

Graham let his thoughts run through his mind. "I'll tell you what," he said. "How about tomorrow, I sit here through practice instead of doing my homework in the library? That way, I'll keep an eye on her, and if I see her doing anything that concerns me, I can say something to her."

"I guess," Kaya said, shrugging. "I think I can take care of myself, but if it makes you feel better, it's fine."

Graham gave his sister a smile. "You know it's my job to look after you, right? What else is a big brother good for?"

"Not much!" Kaya said with a grin. She elbowed Graham gently in the ribs and laughed. They half walked, half wrestled back to the car.

The next day was Friday. After his last class, Graham went to the gym. He got there before Kaya and settled himself on the bleachers. Other kids were there, too, either to watch cheer practice or waiting for wrestling practice later in the afternoon. Graham said hello to some classmates that he recognized and then took out his Calculus textbook. He opened to the page that held his homework problems and worked on them until he saw Kaya emerge from the locker room. She saw him and waved enthusiastically. He waved back.

Soon after, Jill came out, followed by a few other girls. They sat in a wide circle in the middle of the floor around their coach, a young new teacher who had started after Graham became an upperclassman. Her words weren't clear to Graham, but he could hear the cadence of her speech. She was trying to pep up the girls, and it appeared to be working. Soon, the squad was whooping and cheering as they jumped up to grab their pom-poms.

They stood in a line, and the tallest girl, a senior named Missy who Graham had known since freshman year, called out commands. The other cheerleaders called out after her, kicking, and then jumping in the air. It was a sort of choreographed dance, Graham thought, and more organized than it looked. Several times, Missy stopped the girls and gave them further instruction. Then they would start again. This went on for about fifteen minutes, and then the coach turned on some music on a large boom box. Graham didn't even know they still made those things. The music blasted out, and the girls quickly stood in a straight line. The dance began.

Graham was amazed at the coordination that his sister showed within the group. The girls almost looked like they were working as a unit, all of their moves synchronized. And every girl, to a one, had a huge smile on her face. Pom-poms went up, and pom-poms went back down. At certain intervals, the girls would call out words, and then go silent again. Graham found himself smiling at the performance.

After the girls went through their routine three times with the music, the coach turned it off, and the circle reformed. There was more talking, and then the girls split into two groups of six, with two of the older girls left over. Graham watched as three girls from either group knelt on the floor side by side. Then two girls each climbed up on their backs. One of the girls was Jill. Jill took her place with a smile. Then it was time for the last two girls to climb up to the top. The two older girls who were not in the pyramids came and helped boost them up. Graham watched as Kaya was hoisted up on top of Jill and one other girl. The two girls in the middle kept up their smiles, but Graham could definitely see some strain on Jill's face. She did not look comfortable. Soon, the pyramids were complete. Graham kept a close eye on Jill. She stayed amazingly still. Then, very carefully, the two girls on top made their way up on their feet, and there was Graham's sister, standing on top of the world, one foot on the back of each girl below her. She was grinning from ear to ear, but Graham could see her legs shaking. He imagined that his legs would be shaking too if he were that high in the air on top of kneeling teammates.

Suddenly, Kaya looked down at Jill's back. Graham glanced quickly at Jill. Jill was still staring straight ahead, her mouth closed, but her smile looking more like a grimace. Graham looked up. Kaya was still staring at Jill's back, her smile now gone. Then she shook her head.

"Kaya, concentrate!" the coach called out. "Eyes up! Smile! Steady!"

Kaya looked up, eyes straight ahead, and smiled big.

After practice, Graham watched as Kaya said goodbye to her friends and rushed over to him on the bleachers. He was glad that Jill hadn't said anything this time. Kaya would have to feel relieved.

"You looked great out there," he said. "For a minute, though, you looked like you were getting scared. I was worried you'd lose your balance and fall."

Kaya stared at him. "You heard her too?"

Graham got chills. "Heard who?" he asked, afraid of what Kaya was about to say to him.

"Jill," Kaya said. "I can't believe she said that."

"What was it that she said?" Graham asked.

"She said that she hoped I would lose my balance and fall," she said. "I couldn't believe she would say that. And do you know what? I agree with you. I have no idea why no one says anything to her when she says these things. I know I'm one of the new kids, but still. How would they like it if someone kept saying things like that to them? And how bizarre is it that she keeps saying these things right in front of everyone?"

"Wait," Graham said. He was frozen in his seat. He hadn't even begun to put his books away. "When did she say this to you? When you went to get a drink at the fountain?"

Kaya shook her head. "No, dummy," she said. "I just told you. She said she wished I would lose my balance and fall. She said it when we were in the pyramid. During the scariest part, when I was standing. I thought you said you heard her!"

Graham shook his head. "No," he said. "I didn't hear her. I was watching during the pyramid, and I didn't see Jill say anything. Well, she looked sort of like she was struggling. I wonder if she feels like it's too much weight on her back. She was trying to smile, but she couldn't. But at no time did I see or hear her say anything."

Kaya squinted at him. "There's no way you could have missed it. It was really loud. She nearly made me lose my balance, she was saying it so loud."

Graham felt his heart fall. Something was wrong here, but it wasn't with Jill. It was Kaya. She was hearing things that weren't actually being said. "Have you heard anyone else saying weird things recently, Kaya?"

He had learned about mental illness in his AP Psychology class. He was concerned that Kaya might be showing some early symptoms.

Kaya shrugged. "I don't know. I mean, isn't Jill saying mean things to me enough?"

She thought for a moment.

"There was that time in the nurse's office last week when I went to get a Band-Aid for a scab I had scratched off. I was watching her put it on, and suddenly I heard her say, 'I wish you girls would be more careful. At least it's just a scratch. I just hope that a few years from now you're not coming to me with morning sickness.' I thought that was kind of bizarre."

Graham took a deep breath. He knew Mrs. Cazan, the school nurse. She was a timid little woman who was afraid of her own shadow. She appeared to be concerned that her patients were going to turn on her at any moment. That didn't sound like something she would say to anyone, let alone his sweet, innocent little freshman sister.

"C'mon," he said, putting on his jacket and stuffing his books into his backpack. "Let's get going. I still have a bunch of homework to do. I didn't get much done here."

On the way home, he let Kaya play with the radio buttons. She settled on a station with popular music, and she sang and swayed all the way home. When they got there, she jumped out of the car, her backpack on her back, both pom-poms shoved under her arm. She ran inside, and Graham followed slowly. His mother's car was in the driveway, and Graham knew that meant his mother was working from home. He headed to the back room where she'd made her office and knocked on the door. After she called for him to come in, he opened the door.

"Just a minute, sweetie," she said as she typed the end of an email. She hit send with a flourish, and then turned to look at him with a smile. "What's going on, Graham Cracker?"

Graham looked at his mother, her beautiful grin bisecting her face. He wasn't sure what to say. He didn't know how she would receive his words.

"I . . . well, I wanted to talk to you about Kaya ."

Mrs. Reed's smile fell. "What about Kaya?" she asked. "Graham, you look serious as a heart attack. What's wrong?"

Graham sighed and resigned himself to saying what he needed to say. "Mom, I think Kaya might be hearing voices."

KAYA HAD TRIED TO TALK to Jill twice, but both times she had rushed away after practice. She had to ask her why she was saying those things. Was she trying to upset Kaya? What good would that do? Kaya knew Jill wouldn't push her off the pyramid, and she wasn't planning to ever leave her drinks accessible to laxatives. It was so frustrating. But the worst part was that no one else was saying anything. "Can you believe Jill?" Kaya had asked Sarah, the senior.

Sarah shook her head. "I know. She needs better focus. She needs to work on her smile, and her form. If she's not careful, Miss Green will put her on the bottom of the pyramid, and trust me, that's a lot harder." And then she walked away.

Kaya watched after her. Sarah had completely misunderstood what she had been saying. Maybe Kaya was missing something. She'd heard of hazing before. Maybe she was being hazed. She hoped not. She didn't want to be the one the other girls focused on and teased; she wanted to be a leader. Her goal was to eventually become the captain of the team, and she would never haze anyone.

The day after she spoke to Sarah, Kaya walked the halls looking for

Jill. She wanted to pull her aside and ask her why she was giving her such a hard time. But she couldn't find her. She walked into science class and took her seat. She liked science, but there were too many kids in the class. Bailey from cheerleading sat right behind her. She hadn't realized it until the second day of school when she felt a kick on the back of her chair, and she turned around and spotted her.

"What?" Bailey had asked.

"You kicked me."

"Oh, I'm sorry."

Kaya could tell she really was sorry. Bailey seemed nice. She could easily see them becoming friends as the year went on.

"There's no room for my feet under my desk. I have to stretch out. I guess I'll say I'm sorry in advance for any time I do it again. I would move my desk back, but it's too close to the desk behind me. The boy back there keeps kicking me, too."

Kaya had smiled at Bailey. "That's okay," she said. "As long as I know that's why you're doing it. You can put your feet under my chair if you want. I'll just ignore them."

Bailey had smiled back.

On this day, after her search for Jill hadn't panned out and Kaya had taken her seat in front of Bailey, the science teacher started class, and five minutes later, Bailey started singing.

Kaya couldn't believe it. Bailey had a lot of nerve to be singing in class, in front of all of the other students, while the teacher was talking. She turned in her seat to look at Bailey, who only looked back at her questioningly. The singing stopped. Kaya turned back around. Seconds later, the singing started again.

After class, Kaya chased Bailey out of the room. "I can't believe you were singing in class."

Bailey looked confused. "I was singing in class?" she asked. "If I was, I had no idea I was." Her hands went to her face. "Oh, God, that's so embarrassing! Is that why you looked at me? Yikes! I have to be careful. I always have music in my head, but I had no idea I was singing it! If you ever hear me do that again, can you please stop me?"

Kaya nodded. "Of course," she said. "I mean, your voice is really good. But yeah, it's not a good idea to sing in class."

When she got home that afternoon, her mother was sitting on the couch with her work. She glanced up at Kaya and smiled. "Hi, Ky."

Kaya looked at her mother warily as she put down her backpack. "Hi Mom," she said. "What's wrong? Why do you look like that? Is it something about Dad?"

Mrs. Reed shook her head. "No nothing's wrong. I just wanted to let you know that I made an appointment for you to see Dr. Gross tomorrow."

Kaya sat on the couch next to her mother. "But I saw him this summer," she said. "He said I was fine. Why do I have to see him again? Do I need a shot or something?"

"No. . . . I just want to get you a checkup to make sure everything's okay. It's been a stressful year, and I'm just concerned that we all might be taking on more than we can handle. It's just a precaution."

"Oh," Kaya said, still not understanding. "Okay. So what time's the appointment?"

"Right after school."

Kaya's mouth dropped open. "But I have cheer practice right after school. I-I can't miss it!?"

"You can miss one day," Mrs. Reed said. "It will be okay, Kaya. Sometimes, there are more important things than cheerleading. Don't worry. I'll call your coach—what's her name? Miss Green? I'll let her know you'll only be missing one day." She paused. "Ky, I have to be honest with you: Graham and I are concerned about some of the things you've been saying lately. Things about people wanting to hurt you. I just want to make sure that everything's okay. With Dad gone and all . . ."

"There's nothing wrong with me," Kaya said, her throat constricting. "I can't believe Graham told you. Mom, it's not a big deal. Everything's fine."

Mrs. Reed nodded. "Well, if that's the case, we have nothing to worry about. But either way, we're going to the doctor tomorrow, just to be sure. Ky, if anything ever happened to you, I'd never forgive myself . . ."

Kaya blocked out the rest of her mother's words. She wanted to protest. She wanted to fight. She wanted her mother to understand that she was mistaken. There was nothing wrong with her. But when she looked at the pain etched on her mother's face, she gave in. She would go to the doctor the next day. She wouldn't fight it. If her mother needed reassurance, she would give it to her.

Chapter 2

"DR. GROSS DOESN'T THINK IT'S anything serious," Mrs. Reed said. "He thinks that maybe she's taken on too much this year, and she's a bit sleep-deprived."

"But she seems fine except for the weird things she's been hearing," Graham said. "I mean, I still hear her singing in the shower, and she looks happy when she's practicing her cheers, both at school and at home."

Mrs. Reed shrugged. "I don't know what to tell you, Graham," she said. "I asked if he thought she should be seen by a psychiatrist, and he said we should wait. He thought it was best just to give her time to rest and see if this all just stops. That's just the thing; there are no other symptoms. He said if it were a mental illness, we'd probably be seeing mood changes or other concerning behavior. We would have probably seen other things over the years that concerned us, like isolation. She's a social girl. She hasn't withdrawn from her friends. In fact, Cat is upstairs with her right now, listening to CDs. I think I might have heard them dancing around in Kaya's room."

"So how do we help her then?" Graham asked.

"I talked to her about it in the car," his mother said. "I told her about our concerns. I told her I thought it might be a good idea to take a break from cheering for a while, but she got really upset. She's been preparing to be a high school cheerleader for years. All those years of dance classes . . . I couldn't make her quit. I think we just need to wait, to see what happens."

Graham nodded. "I'm gonna go to practice with her for a while. Do you think we need to say anything to the coach?"

Mrs. Reed looked at him, expressionless. "I don't know," she said. "Do you think we should?"

Graham wasn't sure. It would have been helpful to have another adult in the house. Graham would be eighteen in the spring, but he had no experience making adult decisions. "I . . . maybe you could just ask her to keep an eye on her."

Mrs. Reed's eyes were pleading. "Can you just do it, Graham?" she said. "I'm so backed up with work, and I had to take the afternoon off to take Kaya to the doctor. Plus, I just can't handle this right now, you know?" She grasped both sides of her head with her hands and pulled at her hair. "No. Never mind. It's my job to talk to her. I can't ask you to do that. I'm just really overwhelmed right now. I just need some support right now, okay?"

Graham sighed. "Okay." He silently cursed his father. He was supposed to be there. There was too much going on for his mother to take care of everything. "Do you need any help with dinner?"

Mrs. Graham looked at her oldest child and smiled. She cupped his chin with her hand. "You're a good kid, you know that? I think I've got it all under control for now. Why don't you go up and check on Kaya and Cat?"

Graham nodded and trotted up the steps. He knocked on Kaya's door, but the music was playing very loud and no one answered. He knocked again and then turned the knob. He walked in, but the girls still seemed unaware of his presence. Kaya appeared to be teaching Cat one of her cheers, and she was instructing Cat on how to extend her arm properly in the air.

"You have to hold it higher. Here, I'll show you." She took hold of Cat's arm and held it up. She moved it forward. "Yeah, like that."

Suddenly she looked over and saw Graham. "Oh, I didn't hear you come in—I can't believe you just said that, Cat!" she said, dropping their arms.

She shook her head toward Graham. "Everyone I know seems to have stopped keeping things to themselves. Just ignore her. What do you want?"

Graham looked at Cat, who was looking at Kaya, confused.

"Mom's making dinner," Graham said. "She asked me to check on you guys. Is Cat staying for dinner?"

"I'll stay for dinner," Cat said quickly, smiling.

Kaya glared at her. "No surprise," she mumbled. Cat shrugged at her.

"I'll let Mom know," Graham said. He walked out the door.

"Graham, wait," Kaya called, following him out into the hall. She closed the door. "I'm sorry, I had no idea that Cat was gonna say that to you."

Graham lifted a brow. "Say what?"

"Gaham, she couldn't have stated it more clearly." She blinked her eyes, mockingly flirtatious. "'I *love* you, Graham. I hope you love me, too.'" Kaya laughed. "Can you believe she just came out and said it? I've known Cat for four years, and I had no idea she had a crush on you."

Graham shook his head. "Kaya, I have no idea what you're talking about."

Kaya shook her head and pursed her lips. "Graham, you can't tell me you didn't just hear Cat say she loved you, right to your face. Come on."

"I really didn't. I didn't hear any such thing. Kaya—"

Kaya stomped her foot. "Stop it, Graham! I'm not hearing voices. I mean, yeah, I'm hearing voices, but they're not in my head! I heard Cat say she loved you! It was loud and clear! Ugh, what the hell. Graham, I would say you were messing with me, but I don't think you would take it far enough that you'd have Mom take me to the doctor. Maybe you're having problems with your hearing?"

"There's nothing wrong with my hearing," Graham said. He shook his head. "Never mind. Just . . . I don't know. But as far as Cat's concerned, don't worry about it. I don't think she likes me. If she did, I would have sensed it a long time ago. She's always over here. And she's way too young for me."

Kaya grunted. "She said she loves you," she said quietly. "I don't care what you say." She turned and stomped back to her room.

Cheer practice was uneventful the rest of the week. Graham watched carefully throughout the hour, but everything seemed legitimate. Kaya appeared to be enjoying herself, learning new routines, and stretching in new directions. They skipped the pyramid practice all week, so there was no talk of anyone wanting to push his sister off. She gabbed about her friends and classes on the drive home. "My friend Bailey sings all through science class," she said on Friday. "She sits right behind me. You know, it's crazy how many kids are in that class. They only have two science teachers this year instead of three. We're almost on top of each other. So Bailey, she's one of the girls on the cheer team? She's always singing. Right behind me."

"Isn't that distracting?" Graham asked, keeping his eyes on the road.

"It's not too bad," Kaya said. "She sings songs I like, like popular songs. She was singing this one song today by Sarah McLachlan. 'Adia,' I think. I like that song. Bailey's voice isn't as good as Sarah McLachlan's, but it's not bad."

"I've never heard anyone singing in any of my classes," Graham said. "If they did, the teachers would be all over them to stop it, or tell them to leave the room."

Kaya shook her head. "Mrs. Ramsey doesn't say a word, and neither does anyone else. She even calls on Bailey sometimes." Kaya was quiet for a moment. "But you know, the strange thing is, she doesn't stop singing when she's answering questions. Huh. That's kind of weird, don't you think? I guess when she's talking, it's more like humming than singing. I wonder how she does that."

"Wait a minute," Graham said, daring a glance at his sister. "She answers questions and hums at the same time? That's impossible, Ky. Could this be—"

"I told you to stop it!" Kaya shouted. "I'm not hearing things! She sings in class! Why would I imagine something like that? Sometimes she even sings songs I don't even know. And sometimes, she sings the same line over and over. Sometimes she even gets the words wrong."

"I've never seen anyone singing in the halls," Graham challenged.

Kaya rolled her eyes. "She stops at the end of class." She thought some more. "Bailey's in my English class, too. She doesn't sit next to me in that class. She doesn't sing or even hum in there."

Graham pulled the car over to the side of the road. He put it in park and turned to look at Kaya.

"Ky," he said. "I want you to think about it logically, okay? I mean, really, a girl sings all through class, and even when the teacher calls on her. She's still singing, even when she's talking. No one says anything about it. The teacher doesn't tell her to stop. Doesn't that seem strange to you?"

Kaya cocked her head to the side. "Well, yeah," she said, "but stranger things have happened than kids singing in class. Like, Joe Foley asked Katrina Smith out last week. No one saw that coming." Kaya laughed.

Graham couldn't help but smile. Even when she was frustrated, his sister was funny. Then he shook his head. "So then why is no one talking about this Bailey girl singing? I would think you and your friends would talk about it after class. Does anyone talk about it?"

"No," Kaya said defensively. "But maybe they don't care."

"Really?" Graham asked, giving her a skeptical look. "No one cares?"

Kaya was silent. "So what are you trying to say, Graham?" she asked. "The doctor said that I wasn't crazy, but it sounds like you still think I am. What can I do to convince you that I'm not?"

"I have no idea," Graham said. "Maybe you could make a list of strange things that happen that no one else seems to notice. Obviously if anyone had heard Jill say she was going to try to spike your milk with laxative, they would have tried to stop her. And if she had said she wanted you dead, they would have pulled her into the principal's office and had her talk to a therapist. Or the police! And you weren't alone on the pyramid, any of the three times. There was the girl next to Jill. What's her name?"

"Penny."

Graham nodded. "Okay. So here's what I want you to do. I want you to pull Penny aside and ask her what she thinks about what Jill has been saying to you when you're on the pyramid. I promise you, if she really did say anything, Penny would have heard it. If she says she did, ask her why she didn't say anything about it to Jill, or to you. But if she says she didn't hear anything, I want you to consider that maybe Jill didn't say anything."

"So you're saying I imagined it all," Kaya said with a sneer.

"I don't know," Graham said. "I don't think you're doing anything on purpose. And I do believe you're hearing what you say you're hearing. But that doesn't mean that it's really being said. Can you at least try to find out? Just talk to Penny."

Kaya thought about it for a moment. "I'll think about it," she finally said. "If I can convince you that I'm telling the truth, and you stop bugging me about it, it would be worth it."

"I love the pad Thai here," Kaya said excitedly as she followed Graham and her mother across the threshold of the restaurant. "Mom, can I get a Thai iced tea?"

Mrs. Reed shook her head. "There's so much caffeine in those; you wouldn't come down for at least a week."

A sly smile appeared on Kaya's face. "So can I get a Pepsi instead?" Her mother nodded.

Graham looked at his sister and returned her smile. She had just played their mother. Mrs. Reed hardly ever agreed to let her children have caffeinated beverages. Kaya was becoming a clever schemer. He watched her as she hummed and folded her cloth napkin like origami. She seemed so normal and happy. No one else would ever think there was anything possibly wrong with her. She was just a normal happy kid. Maybe Graham was overthinking. She'd always had an active imagination. Maybe she was creating stories in her head, and they just seemed real to her. He had to back off a little, not worry so much.

The waiter approached their table. "Would you all like some hot tea?" he asked. Everyone nodded. The waiter reached across and poured the tea into their cups. As he reached toward Mrs. Reed, his arm brushed against Kaya's hand. "Oh, excuse me."

Kaya looked up at him and smiled. "It's okay," she said kindly.

The waiter walked away, and Kaya brought the cup to her mouth and took a small sip. "That's really too bad."

"What's too bad?" Mrs. Reed asked.

Kaya shrugged. "What the waiter said."

Graham felt a churning in his stomach. "What the waiter said?" he asked. "All I heard was him asking if we wanted tea, and then he said excuse me."

Kaya nodded. "Yeah, right after that. He said his feet hurt. He's been on them for hours. He wants to sit down. I almost invited him to sit with us."

Mrs. Reed looked up from her menu. "What?" she asked. "I didn't hear him say that." She looked at Graham, her voice getting lower. "Did you, Graham?"

Graham shook his head.

Kaya shook her head too. "Oh no," she said. "No. I did not make this up! He said that! Didn't you see the look on his face? His feet hurt!"

She looked like she might start to cry out of frustration.

Mrs. Reed reached out her hand and put it on top of Kaya's.

"I don't think you made it up, Kaya," she said. "I just . . . maybe you saw the look on his face, and you thought that it looked like his feet were hurting, and you thought that maybe if it were you, you'd want to sit down if your feet hurt."

"But if that's the case, then you think I'm hearing voices!" Her tone was becoming a whine. "Mom, is there really something wrong with me? Why does no one else hear the things I hear? I don't feel crazy! I just hear stuff. It's not even big stuff. Just little stuff. Well, except for the Jill stuff. But if I were gonna hear voices, I don't think this is the kind of stuff I would hear!"

Mrs. Reed bit her lower lip and shook her head.

"I don't know what to say," she said. "I—I don't think you're crazy, Kaya. You're not doing anything crazy. You're not hurting anyone. You just hear weird stuff. Up until now, I didn't even know it was going on. I just knew what Graham had told me." She sighed. "But I am concerned about you. Please, consider taking some time off from cheer and getting some rest."

"No!" Kaya exclaimed, pounding her fist on the table. "I'm not gonna stop cheer! Mom! It's my thing! I love it! If I stop cheer, *then* I'll go crazy. You know that! What if I just rest tomorrow instead? I have plans with Rayna. I can cancel them and sleep late. I can read and watch TV. Please, Mom!"

Mrs. Reed glanced at Graham and then back at Kaya.

"Fine," she said. "Fine. Rest tomorrow. But if this keeps up, Kaya, I'm calling your doctor again and insisting on seeing a psychiatrist to see what's going on. Do you understand?"

Kaya's brow furrowed. "You're talking like I'm in trouble," she said sullenly. "Like I'm doing this on purpose. Mom. Please. You know me. I don't lie. I don't make things up."

Mrs. Reed closed her eyes for several seconds. As she opened them, the waiter appeared at the table.

"Can I take your orders?" he asked.

Graham looked at the waiter's face closely. He was focusing on Mrs. Reed as she gave her order. But as he turned to look at Kaya, Graham could swear he saw the man grimace. Maybe his feet did hurt. He gave the waiter his order, then turned to Kaya.

"Did he say anything else about his feet, or anything else?" Graham asked.

Kaya shook her head.

"Did you hear him say anything else? He asked us all for our orders, and then he repeated them back to us. Exciting."

Graham nodded and then took a sip of his lukewarm tea.

After school on Monday, Graham sat on the bleachers again and watched Kaya walk out of the locker room, side by side with another girl. It was the girl who had been on the pyramid next to Jill. Penny. Her name was Penny. Graham let out a sigh of relief. Kaya was doing what he had asked her to do. He would check in with her after practice to see what she found out.

The girls were back to practicing their pyramid, as well as other lifts and flips. Graham watched closely as Kaya was hefted to the top of the pile and then stood up tall. The entire process appeared to go off without a hitch.

After practice, Kaya came running over to Graham.

"Let's go," she said. She grabbed her jacket and started to trot toward the door. Graham had to hustle to keep up with her.

"Kaya," he called out to her. "Wait up."

Kaya slowed down, her back still to Graham. She waited for him to catch up. Then she turned to look at him. He could see a tear developing in the corner of one eye.

"She had no idea what I was talking about. She said that she didn't doubt that Jill might think of something like knocking someone off a pyramid, but she never said anything out loud. I felt like such an idiot! I had to pull back and make it seem like I was exaggerating. I laughed and told her that I didn't mean that she said it, I just meant that she might have thought it."

She started again toward the car.

"Maybe I *am* crazy!" she yelled back at him. "I mean, it was clear as day.

She said she wished I would die. But she never said it, Graham. She never said anything at all. That's it. I'm cuckoo. It's all over for me. Might as well lock me away at the funny farm before I do anything dangerous."

She opened the passenger door and got inside. By the time Graham got in on his side, she was sobbing, her face in her hands.

CHAPTER 3

"KAYA, WHAT DO YOU WANT to do?" Graham said as she watched his sister cry beside him.

Kaya looked up, her eyes red, tears flowing down her cheeks. "About what?"

"About all of this," he said, gesturing toward her. "About what you said. About hearing things that no one else hears."

"What *is* there to do?" Kaya asked. "I guess I just have to figure out what to do about all of this."

"Maybe we should have Mom make that appointment with a psychiatrist, to see if they could help you."

Kaya shook her head. "No . I just need to figure out how to know when something's real and something's not. I have to look at people when they're talking to me. If I hear something that doesn't sound right, I have to either check it out and see if anyone else heard it, or else just ignore it."

"Do you think you can do that?" Graham asked. "I mean, you couldn't do it before."

"But before I thought it was real," Kaya said. "It didn't even occur to me to check their lips. Now I know it's not. Graham, I told you, I don't feel like there's anything wrong with me. This doesn't happen all the time. Most of the time, things are normal."

"What do you think brings it on?"

"Nothing!" Kaya exclaimed, hitting her hands against her sides. "I can't think of anything. It happens at different times. I don't feel tired, or stressed, or confused. None of that. I'm just going along with my day like I usually do, and then I hear weird things. But it just sounds like the person next to me is talking to me. Nothing out of the ordinary. But when they talk, they say things that they wouldn't say normally. It's like all of their filters are gone."

Graham sighed. He turned the key in the ignition. "If you think you can do this, I won't say anything to Mom. But if it seems like things are getting worse, or you can't control it, all deals are off. I talk to Mom, and we get you professional help."

Kaya closed her eyes. "I just don't want anyone else to know about this, okay? Can we keep it just in the family?"

Graham nodded.

"Okay, then. So when I go back to school, I'll be more careful. And maybe, if you see me in the halls and stuff, you can look out for me."

Graham smiled. "Kaya, I'm your big brother. I always look out for you. And I'll be at practice every day, doing my homework."

"There's a basketball game on Tuesday," Kaya said. "It's at Florence High. Can you go?"

"I guess," Graham said. "I'm not much of a basketball fan, but I do like to watch the cheerleaders!"

Kaya laughed. "Really? Which ones?"

Graham grinned. "My sister, dummy!"

"Oh," Kaya said. "I thought maybe you were thinking of Bailey, or Sandy. They're really pretty. Most of the guys like to look at them."

"I haven't noticed," Graham said, and he grinned. He stopped at a red light to peer over at Kaya. Her face was still damp from tears. He pulled a napkin out of the console between the seats and reached out to wiped the tears from her cheek. "I guess I just haven't looked close enough."

Kaya paused for a moment. Then she looked up and smiled. "Because you like Gina Simpson?"

Graham's mouth dropped open. "How did you know that?" he asked. "I haven't told anyone!"

Kaya looked at him mischievously. "I don't know, I guess a sister can tell these things just by looking. Graham, she's really nice. And she's cute. And she's smart. Have you told her you like her?"

Graham shook his head. "I haven't got up the nerve," he said. "I mostly only see her in AP and honors classes, and she always has her nose in a book or a notebook. I—I think she'd probably say yes." He glanced at Kaya quickly before he started across the intersection. "Don't you think?"

Kaya shrugged. "I can't see why not. I think she'd be perfect for you. You're not for everyone, Graham. I mean, girls like Bailey and Sandy couldn't keep up a conversation with you. The first time you said the word *literature* to either one of them, their eyes would go dull." She laughed. "Yeah, you need a special kind of girl."

"I'm not sure if that's a vote of confidence or not," Graham said. He was trying to make light conversation with Kaya, but it didn't feel light at all. His sister was going through something he didn't understand. He vowed to go to the library over the weekend to learn more about hearing voices.

On Saturday afternoon, Graham left his mother cleaning the house, and Kaya watching movies on the DVD player with Cat, and drove to the town library. He asked the librarian to direct him to books and journals on psychiatry. He started with the Diagnostic and Statistical Manual, DSM-IV, the bible for mental health definitions and symptoms that they had used in his AP class. He looked through the index for auditory hallucinations.

The definition of schizophrenia or psychotic disorders indicated that a person would display delusions, hallucination, disorganized speech, grossly disorganized or catatonic behavior, and negative symptoms, such as appearing flat of emotions, and isolating. Kaya had the auditory hallucination but none of the other symptoms. Aside from the voices, she appeared totally normal. The text said that in order to be diagnosed with these illnesses, a person had to display at least two symptoms.

He looked for any other disorders that could cause voices. Kaya also didn't have the symptoms of bipolar disorder or depression. In the medical texts, he found information about people with migraines or brain tumors sometimes having hallucinations, but Kaya rarely had headaches. It seemed unlikely that she had a brain tumor, but if things didn't get better, he might mention that possibility to his mother. There were a few other possible causes, but they were all diseases of old age, something he could easily rule out. After two hours of research, Graham closed all of his books, packed his notebook into his backpack, and returned the texts to the shelving cart.

Graham entered his house and found the first floor quiet and empty. Upstairs, he confirmed Kaya wasn't home. His mother was in her room, her legs stretched out on her bed, her back propped up on her pillows. She was looking through a pile of open mail. She wore a fixed look of concentration as she stared at papers sitting on her lap. She looked up when Graham came in and tried to smile. The smile didn't reach her eyes.

"I didn't hear you come in."

Graham sat on the edge of the bed. "Where's Kaya?"

"She and Cat got bored and decided to take the bus down to the shopping plaza. I guess the movie I got from Netflix wasn't enticing enough. By the way, next time you go out, can you drop it in the mailbox?"

Graham nodded. "You looked totally stressed out, Mom," he said. He pointed to the mail. "Is that all bills?"

Mrs. Reed nodded. "Some of them are coming due, but I have to figure out which ones I can safely pay before payday. I guess I'll have to deal with a few late fees, but what else am I supposed to do?"

"You could figure out how to contact Dad and tell him you need money," Graham said, trying to keep the contempt out of his voice. "It's the least he could do."

Mrs. Reed closed her eyes and sighed. "I have no idea how to even start to find him," she said. "He said he was hitting the road, but he never said which road. I think he's probably trying to figure out where to land. I still can't take it in. All those years, and he seemed like he was happy. I just don't know . . ."

"I don't know either, Mom," Graham said. "If I could find him myself, I would. And I'd knock him around a little until he came to his senses." He looked at his hands. "I mean, I'm almost grown, but Kaya, she still needs both of her parents. She's been doing so well, but . . ." He stopped himself. He had promised to wait on talking about Kaya's voices with his mother.

"But, you know, maybe she's putting on a happy face for us, so we don't feel bad."

Mrs. Reed bit her lower lip. It was a habit she had picked up ever since her husband had left six months earlier.

"I know, Graham," she said. "I think we've all been trying to put on a brave face. Maybe we should all talk about it more as a family. But I've been so busy trying to work and run the household all by myself. I always thought that your father didn't do much around the house, but I discounted how much having a second adult here made a difference."

"Mom," Graham said softly, reaching out to touch her arm. "I'm pretty much an adult. I can help. I've told you that."

This time, Mrs. Reed's smile was genuine. "Graham, you've been helping me. A lot. More than you know. You've been a wonderful brother to Kaya, and you offer to help me all the time. And the fact that you've been driving Kaya home from cheer practice, and even staying there with her the last few weeks, that's been amazing. She knows that you're there for her, and that means everything." She laughed. "When I was Kaya's age, my two older brothers teased me mercilessly. I protested, but deep down inside, I knew they wouldn't have teased me if they didn't love me. But Kaya doesn't have to figure out if you love her. You're right there for her."

She put her hand over his and squeezed.

Graham hoped that his mother was right. "Mom, I can get a job," he said. "So I can help out around here. It won't get in the way of my schoolwork. I can work on weekends, and maybe even some nights. I only have one term left after this one. I could work at the plaza, or even do some custodial work in town. I know they're always looking for people to work in the evenings."

Mrs. Reed shook her head. "Graham, I appreciate the offer. I really do. I know you want to help more, but you don't need to. We'll be okay. I'm just trying to get organized. We're not gonna have our heat or lights turned off or anything. I have to work out a budget. I'll see if Grandma can help me. She used to do the books for Grandpa's business. She's pretty good at it."

Graham nodded. "But if it looks like things are getting tight, will you promise to let me know?"

"I will," Mrs. Reed said. She looked at his backpack. "Did you get what you needed at the library?"

"Not really," Graham said. "I'm doing some research for my science class. We're on a genetics unit. I was trying to find information on diseases that can be passed down from generation to generation. Do we have anything like that in our family? You know, like a tendency toward diabetes, heart disease, or mental illness?"

He hoped that he had presented his lie in a way that his mother would buy it.

Mrs. Reed thought for a moment. "My grandmother had some sort of thyroid disorder," she said. "She had to have it removed, and take medicine for the rest of her life. She did live to be eighty-six, though, so it didn't seem to slow her down at all. My paternal grandfather, Grandpa Tony, had liver cancer. But neither of my parents or my brothers have had signs of cancer."

"What about Dad's family?"

Mrs. Reed looked at him. "What are you going to do with all this information?"

Graham shrugged. "I think we're gonna look at what our family members had, and then see if any of them are genetically based. We don't have to share the information with the class. It's all for our own knowledge."

"Oh," his mother said. "Well, I'm not sure. Your grandparents are in fairly good health. They're lacking a bit in the personality department, but that doesn't really count. I'm not sure about his grandparents. I think most of them died when he was young. I do remember there being some talk of someone in the family having depression. That's one that you might check on. I don't remember who it was, though, but I think that does run in the family. I sometimes wonder if that's what made your father feel like running."

She looked back down at her pile of bills and started to flip through them again.

Graham thought that it might be time to let it go. "I think that's enough," he said. "I can go with the liver cancer, thyroid, and depression. I'll let you know if I find anything out. I'm gonna go get a snack. Do you want me to take anything out of the freezer for dinner?"

"You can look in there and decide between ground beef and chicken if you want," she said. "I'll be down in about a half hour to cook something up."

On Tuesday, Graham steeled himself for a late night. Kaya would meet with the cheer team after school, and then they would take the bus to Florence High for the basketball game. Graham would do his homework in the library before heading over to the game. His friend Chet joined him in the library.

"If you want, I can go with you," Chet said. "I don't think I'd want to sit in the bleachers at a strange school by myself. I wouldn't want to do it at our own school either. I mean, I don't hate basketball or anything."

Graham shrugged. "Sure. I can drive you home after if you want. Yeah, it'll be nice to have company. You should see these girls. Well, you're going to, but I mean, they're really good. It's not just cheering. It's dancing. It's a whole sport on its own. And Kaya says everyone's hot for Bailey and Sandy. They're sophomores. Maybe you'll like one of them."

Chet laughed. "I think those girls might take one look at me and put the big L on their foreheads." He demonstrated with his own thumb and index finger. "Loser! I've seen it before. It's okay, though. In the end, I've got better prospects than them. When we come back for our tenth reunion, they'll be sorry they never gave me the time of day, especially when they see my expensive Rolex."

Graham smiled. "Okay. Let's just get through our calculus, and then we can go. I brought snacks for the game."

At Florence, they found an area in the bleachers that contained members of the away school's fans and got comfortable. Graham put his puffy jacket under his butt to keep the hardwood from annoying his tailbone. Both teams were on the court, taking practice shots. Graham noticed one member of the opposing team was far over six feet tall, and he had the shadow of a mustache. He rubbed his own upper lip and felt the thickening but still fine hair. If his father had been around, he would have asked him about starting to shave, but as it was, he was putting it off. It wasn't his top priority.

After a few minutes, a whistle blew, and the players went to their benches. The cheerleaders from both teams ran out onto the floor. The Florence High girls went first. Loud, frantic music came over the loudspeaker system, and one girl stepped in front of the others and started to dance. The others started behind her. These girls were dancing fast and tight. It was hard to follow, but amazing to watch. The music stopped, and then it was Wisteria High's turn.

The girls stood stone still. The music started. It was a slower, more melodic tune. The girls began with more fluid motion. They all maintained their smiles throughout the dance. Graham watched Kaya as she took each step, made each turn, her smile genuine. He felt happy for her. This was where she always wanted to be. He was glad she was pursuing her dream.

The game dragged on throughout the first half. Graham had been hopeful that each eight-minute quarter would fly by, but the clock stopped so often that each period was more like twenty minutes. Stoppages were boring. The only relief was when the girls on either side got up to cheer. Now Graham understood the theory of cheerleading: keeping the crowd engaged through the boring moments so they wouldn't walk out or fall asleep.

Finally, halftime arrived, and the players receded to their locker rooms. Again, the cheerleaders took turns doing routines. Florence went first. The girls took the opportunity to show off their gymnastic skills, doing flips and backbends, along with cartwheels and lifts. Then Wisteria went to work. Again, their dance was slower and more relaxed. At the end of their routine, they all lined up and then split into their groups for their pyramids. Graham watched with anticipation as the pyramids grew, Kaya was hoisted to the top of hers, and a teammate handed her up her pompoms. She stood tall and proud with a huge smile. She lifted her pompoms in the air, and the girls started their well-rehearsed cheer.

Suddenly, something changed.

CHEERING IN FRONT OF AN audience was everything that Kaya had dreamed it would be. As she cheered, their enthusiasm grew, in turn making her more excited. The cheers and routines were going off just as Miss Green had taught them. Kaya could see a pleased expression on her coach's face as she watched her team in action. Kaya liked and admired Miss Green, so she felt pleased, too. She didn't have to fake her smiles as she bobbed her pompoms up and down to the music. It was fun to stand on the sidelines during the game and start cheers during stoppages in play. Kaya had a chance to look up in the crowd and find Graham sitting there with his friend Chet. She wasn't able to wave, as she was in the middle of a cheer, but she did send him a big smile.

When halftime came, everyone cleared the floor and went back to the girls' locker room. There, they stood in a huddle. "Girls, you're doing so great!" Miss Green said with a smile. "I'm so proud of you! You've been working so hard together as a team for the last few weeks, and it shows. Your moves are tight, and your smiles are bright. The girls from Florence are going out first to do their halftime routines, and then we'll be up. Are you all ready?" All the girls held up their pompoms and made whooping sounds in agreement. "Great!" Miss Green said. "The team can feel your energy! We're ahead, and a lot of that has to do with you! Keep it up. I know you girls will do great. Okay, hands in. On three, 'Go, Wisteria!' One, two, three!"

"Go, Wisteria!" the girls called out. Then they jumped up and down and shouted.

When the time came, they all filed back out to the court and lined up for their choreographed dance. It went perfectly. Kaya was worried about the last part of the dance, as the team had been struggling to get it right for the last few days. But it came together just right, and she could hear the crowd cheer. Now, it was time for the frosting on the cake.

They lined up in groups of six, and two groups of three got down on the ground on their hands and knees. Then came the second row, with Jill and Penny climbing up on Kaya's pyramid. Lastly, Sarah came and helped Kaya climb up to the top of the group. She got on her knees and slowly started to stand. She felt her knees wobbling but then she got her balance. She smiled.

"Just fall," Jill said below her out of nowhere. "Just fall over, Kaya. It won't take much. Topple over, and hit the floor. Then it will be my turn to be on top."

Sarah handed Kaya her pompoms, and Kaya held them high. She ignored the words she had just heard from Jill and moved ahead with her stance. It was just the voices. They couldn't hurt her. Just as the cheer was about to start, she heard Jill's voice again.

"I can push you," she said. "I'm gonna do it this time. Get ready to hit the floor."

Kaya looked down below her. "No!" she shouted. She started to panic. She felt herself get angry. She shouted again. "No!" And that's when she started to fall. She was on top of the pyramid, but moments later, she was on the ground. And her body screamed out in pain.

Chapter 4

GRAHAM RUSHED DOWN TO THE basketball court and tried to get to his sister. A crowd had already gathered around her. The basketball coach and the cheerleading coach were crouched on the floor by Kaya's side, and the basketball coach shouted instructions to one of his players. The player ran out of the gym, most likely to call an ambulance. Graham pushed through the other cheerleaders and players, who had just come out of the locker room for the second half, and finally got to Kaya.

"Kaya!" he called out.

Kaya's head turned toward him. She was stretched out on the floor, tears on her face.

"Graham!" she cried, reaching out a hand toward him. The cheerleading coach moved away and let him kneel next to his sister. "Graham! I fell from the pyramid!"

"I know," Graham said, taking her outstretched hand. "What hurts?"

"My ankle," Kaya said, "and my wrist. I put out my arm to try to stop the fall. I-I can't believe she finally did it!"

The cheerleading coach looked at Kaya. "Did what?"

Kaya looked at her coach. "Knock me off the pyramid. She's been wanting to do it for a long time."

Miss Green looked horrified. "Who knocked you off?"

Graham quickly turned to the coach. "I'm sorry," he said. "I don't know your name."

"Miss Green," the coach said. "I'm the coach. I assume you're Kaya's brother. I've seen you watching practice in the bleachers. I—I spoke to your mother a few weeks ago. What does she mean, someone's been wanting to knock her off the pyramid for a long time?"

Graham shook his head and moved Miss Green out of Kaya's earshot. "Kaya's been having some issues lately," he said. "That's why my mom wanted us to watch out for her. She's been under a lot of stress. She's been saying some . . . strange things."

Miss Green nodded. "Kaya told me about your father," she said, sympathy showing in her eyes. "I imagine that must take a toll on a young girl. But she seemed to be adjusting so well."

"Yeah, she's been doing great for a long time," Graham said. "I'll have to let my mom know that she's struggling again. I saw her fall. I didn't see anyone knock her down."

"Graham!" Kaya called out. "Come back. Please."

Graham looked solemnly at Miss Green and then went back to his sister's side. He took her hand again. "I'm right here, Kaya."

Kaya looked up at his face. "She said she was gonna do it. She specifically said, 'I'm gonna do it this time.' I tried to ignore her, like I've been doing. I tried to believe that it wasn't real. But then she did it! She knocked me off!"

Graham shook his head. "Kaya, I was watching the whole time," he said. "I didn't see anyone do anything to make you fall. You just lost your balance."

Kaya shook her head. "No! I didn't! I mean, I did, but only because Jill made me. She twisted her back or something. I don't know exactly what she did, but she made me fall."

Graham wasn't sure how to respond. He could tell that Kaya believed with all of her heart that her teammate had caused the fall. "Kaya," he said. "I'll go with you to the hospital. Chet's here, so I'll ask him to drive my car home. I have to call Mom. Can you stay here with Miss Green until I call her? But Kaya, don't say anything else to her about what happened on the pyramid, okay? Let's talk to Mom first. She'll know what to do."

Kaya nodded meekly and let her head rest on the floor. Graham pulled his sweatshirt up above his head, bunched it up, and put it under Kaya's head. "Thanks." She turned her head away from him. "You don't believe me, do you? You think this was just one of those voices things. Yes, I did hear Jill say she was gonna do it. She told me to get ready to hit the floor. That's why I yelled out before I fell. I was trying to stop her! But she didn't listen. I knew I was gonna fall! Graham!" She sighed. "You have to believe me!" She started to cry again.

At that moment, the paramedics came through the gym door, pushing a stretcher. "Kaya, we'll talk later. I have to call Mom real quick. Then I'll be back. The ambulance guys will take care of you. You'll be okay."

He stood and ran toward the hallway where he found a payphone by the main entrance of the school. He called his home number and was relieved when his mother picked up the phone. He told her about the accident, and she promised to meet him at the hospital as soon as she could. He hung up the phone and ran back to the gym.

The paramedics were loading Kaya onto the stretcher as Graham approached. He stood next to one of them until he looked at him. "Is she doing okay?"

The paramedic looked at him and smiled. "Are you her boyfriend?" he asked.

"No," Graham said. "I'm her older brother. How is she?"

"She'll be okay," the paramedic said. "It looks like a couple of sprains, and maybe a bruised tailbone. We'll get her to emergency and they'll get some pictures to make sure. Are your parents here?"

"Our mom will meet us there," Graham said. "I need to go with her, okay?"

The paramedic nodded. "No problem, man. Nice looking out for your little sister. I never had a little sister. Just an older one. Left home after high school and never came back. Could have used her advice sometimes." He walked back over to Kaya and kneeled next to her, talking to her softly.

The second parametric approached him. "You're the brother?" Graham nodded. "Do you know if she has any allergies?"

"Penicillin," Graham said. "Nothing else that I know of."

The paramedic nodded and made a mark on the paper on his clipboard. "Any medical problems that you know of?"

Graham hesitated. He wasn't sure if he should mention the voices. There was that small concern that it could be a brain tumor, like he'd read about in the library. But the paramedic didn't need to know that. "No."

"Okay. Are you riding with us?" Graham nodded. "Get your jacket. We'll be heading out in a minute or so."

Graham nodded and climbed the bleachers.

"Is she gonna be okay?" Chet asked nervously when he reached him. "Man, she fell from pretty high. I thought for sure she was a goner."

"Me too." Graham sighed. "She's hurt, but it's just minor," he said. He took his keys from his pocket. "Can you drive my car home? I'd really be grateful."

Chet nodded and took the keys. "Call me later and let me know she's okay," he said. He put on his jacket. "I'm kinda glad I don't have to watch the second half of this game, but not that it came about this way." He gave Graham's arm a squeeze and then turned to leave.

Graham pulled on his own jacket and returned to the center of the floor. Other observers looked like they were starting to get bored. Graham caught sight of Jill standing off to the side of the court by herself, pom-poms dangling from her hands. Her forehead was wrinkled, and she was gnawing on her knuckles. Graham couldn't tell if it was a look of concern or of guilt. It had to be concern. There was no sign that Jill had done anything to cause Kaya's fall.

The paramedics started to collect their tools and then pushed the stretcher toward the hallway. Graham followed behind. "Where's Graham?" he heard Kaya say to the team.

"I'm right here," Graham said, trotting to walk alongside the stretcher. "Mom's gonna meet us at the ER. We'll make sure they take care of you."

Kaya reached her arm out, and Graham took her hand. "Everything hurts," she moaned. "And I feel like such an idiot. All of those people, watching me fall!" She shook her head. "For the rest of high school, I'll be known as the cheerleader who fell off the pyramid during her first game. Maybe even after high school. I'll be famous at Wisteria High, and Florence High for that matter, for the rest of my life!"

I'd rather have you be known as that, Graham thought, *than as the girl who went nuts, accused someone of knocking her off the pyramid, and then threw herself to the floor.*

The ride to the hospital was short. All rides through Wisteria, and its neighboring town of Florence, were short. They were small towns, even compared to other small towns. Soon, Kaya's stretcher was being pushed through the main doors and directed to a holding room. A nurse came to her side, immediately in action. A moment later, Mrs. Reed entered the room. "Kaya!" she said. She ran to her side. "Are you okay?"

At the first glance of her mother, Kaya started to cry anew. "Mom! I fell! It was so scary! I thought I was gonna fall on my head and die!" She sniffed.

Mrs. Reed took her hand. "I'm here now, sweetheart," she said softly. "You're gonna be okay."

Kaya's lower lip trembled. "It was Jill!" she said. "She did it! No one believes me! I knew she was gonna do it. She's been telling me. I really tried to ignore it like it wasn't real, but doesn't this prove that it was real? Mom, I'm not imagining the voices!"

Mrs. Reed looked at Graham, horror in her eyes.

"Kaya," she said, composing her expression quickly before turning back. "We'll talk about that later. Now, we just need to make sure you're okay. Once we know that, we'll talk more."

The doctor came into the room.

"Hello, Kaya," she said. "I'm Dr. Bellows. I hear you took a fall." She looked at the chart the nurse had been working on. "Your wrist and ankle hurt, and also your butt." She smiled. "I'll take a look, and then we'll take some X-rays."

She examined Kaya from head to toe, even places that Kaya had not complained about. When she was finished, she waved Graham and Mrs. Reed closer and spoke to the whole family.

"I don't think there are any fractures, but we won't take any chances. I'll order wrist, ankle, and pelvic X-rays. Mrs. Reed, you can accompany her down to X-ray. After she comes back, we'll talk some more."

"Dr. Bellows," Mrs. Reed said, her hand on her neck and her voice laced with anxiety. "Would it be okay if I speak to you for a moment in the hall?"

Dr. Bellows nodded and led Mrs. Reed outside the room.

Kaya turned to Graham. "What's she gonna tell her?" she asked. "She's gonna tell her I'm hearing voices, isn't she? Graham, if they think I'm crazy, they'll put me in the hospital! I swear, I'm not crazy! Please, tell them I'm not crazy!"

Graham bit his lower lip. He was picking up his mother's nervous tic.

"Kaya, no one thinks you're crazy," he said. "We're all just . . . worried about you, that's all. Can't you see how it looks to everyone else? I've watched you do the pyramid at least ten times. I've never seen Jill say or do anything out of the ordinary, even when you say that she did. What am I supposed to think? I want to believe you. I mean, I do believe that you heard what you heard. I just don't know where it came from. But what I think is that it came from your own head. From what I've read about voices, they sound as real as if you were hearing someone speak. They know some stuff about what part of the brain causes them, but so far, they don't have the greatest treatment to make them stop. All they can do is try to make them go away by giving people medicine that blocks them."

"I don't want to take medicine!" Kaya protested. "I'm not sick! Grandma takes like eight pills every day. But she's seventy-eight. I'm only fourteen! And I don't think I need any medicine. I was able to go for a long time without letting it bother me. I can do that again!"

"Kaya," Graham said gently. "You just don't get it. You could have been really hurt. What if you *had* fallen on your head? You could have died, or ended up with a really bad head injury. You could have broken your spine and ended up paralyzed. Can't you see how serious this is? What if it *was* voices? What if you thought that Jill was saying she was going to hurt you, and it freaked you out so bad that you panicked, and you fell on your own? Doesn't that scare you at all, that maybe you're the one that caused this in the first place?"

Kaya stared at him, her lips pursed. Then she turned away. Mrs. Reed came back into the room, smiling.

"Someone will be coming in soon to wheel you down to X-ray," she said. "I'm hoping this goes quickly so we don't have to be here all night." She looked at Graham. "While we're gone, you can wait in the waiting room." She handed him some bills. "You can get some food from the machines if you want, or you can go to the cafeteria."

"What did you say to the doctor?" Kaya insisted.

Mrs. Reed kept her smile in place. "Kaya, I just told her some of my concerns, that's all."

Kaya nodded. "You told her that I'm crazy. That I hear voices. Mom, are they gonna lock me up? I'm not hurting anyone! I just want to go home!"

Mrs. Reed shook her head and took Kaya's good hand. "Kaya, no one's gonna lock you up. I just told Dr. Bellows that I was worried about you, and the fact that you got hurt. I'm worried that you might get hurt again. I'm scared, Kaya. I have one job, and it's to keep you safe. If I can't keep you safe, I fail. So I asked Dr. Bellows to make a referral to the psychiatric department, so you can see someone, and we can talk about how we can make these voices stop, once and for all."

Kaya closed her eyes. "They're not gonna stop, Mom! They're not voices! They're real!" She inhaled deeply and then sighed. She shook her head. "Why should I even bother? No one believes me! Don't you think I know myself? I would know if something was wrong."

"Kaya," Graham said, "I've actually read that most people with mental illness don't really have good insight into what's going on with them. That's what's so tricky about it. Mental illness fools the person who has it into believing that it's all real. That's why it's important for the people who love you to make sure you have the treatment you need. To keep you safe."

"If you want to keep me safe," Kaya said softly, almost too controlled, "you'll do something to stop Jill. If no one does anything about her, someone else is gonna get hurt. You just watch. You'll see. I bet you anything, at the next cheerleading practice, Jill will be right up there, on top of my pyramid. And she'll look really happy. And you know why? Because she did what she had to do to get her way. Trust me. That's what's gonna happen." She closed her eyes, as if trying to shut out the rest of the world.

Mrs. Reed quickly pulled Graham out of the room. "Is it just me," she said quietly, "or does it sound like she's starting to get paranoid, too?"

Graham felt as if something had just grabbed his heart and squeezed. "Paranoid?"

Mrs. Reed nodded. "Dr. Bellows asked me if she had any symptoms besides the voices, and I told her no. She told me to watch out for delusions, like having thoughts about things that aren't really happening. Paranoia is a kind of delusion. I think Kaya's really stuck on this idea that Jill's trying to hurt her. It's getting bigger and bigger. She believes it so much, it might be that's why she fell. Graham, I really think we need to get her on medication now before it gets worse." She shook her head. "I really wanted to believe it was just stress." She looked down, took a few breaths, and then lifted her head. "But I don't think it is. Graham, I'm afraid there might be a long road ahead of us, and I'm gonna really need you to help me. Do you think we can work together to help Kaya get well?"

Graham glanced into the holding space. Kaya was still lying still with her eyes closed tightly, her good hand gripping the bed rail so hard, it was turning white. He turned back to his mother and nodded.

"I'll help you," he said. "I love Kaya. I want her to be okay. I just hope that whatever we try, it will help her soon. I hate to see her feeling so scared and alone."

Chapter 5

"I CAN'T BELIEVE JILL DIDN'T get the top of the pyramid," Kaya said. She and Graham were sitting on the bleachers, watching the cheerleading team practice. It had been two weeks since the accident, and Kaya had her crutches wedged into the space beside her. "She doesn't look very happy."

"No, she doesn't," Graham agreed. "She probably assumed the spot was hers when it opened. Maybe Miss Green had other ideas."

"Bailey's much better than Jill," Kaya said. "It makes sense." She looked like she wanted to say more, but she held it back.

Graham could tell that Kaya was trying hard. "So how is it going with the side effects?" he asked. "Are you still feeling lightheaded?"

Kaya shook her head. "No, not anymore. I'm sleeping better. The doctor said that most of the side effects would wear off in a few weeks. My mouth is still dry, though." She touched her tongue to her lips as if to demonstrate.

Graham nodded. "Do you think they're helping at all?"

Kaya shrugged. "Who knows? Sometimes I went weeks without anything weird happening anyway before I started them. The jury's still out on if the meds are doing anything." She sighed. "I hate being on meds. I feel like I'm really crazy." She looked at her feet. "Graham, do you think I'm crazy? Please, be honest with me. Don't hold back."

Graham had to think for a few moments before answering. Kaya deserved to hear the truth from him. "No," he said firmly. "No. I don't think you're crazy, but I also don't know what crazy is. When I think of crazy, I think of old Aunt Connie, and how she used to talk so much about nothing, and then interrupt people when they were talking, starting new conversations. Remember those ridiculous outfits she used to wear? But that's just what comes up in my mind. Aunt Connie wasn't mentally ill. She was eccentric. She just had a way about her that could be a little bit much. Mental illness can mean a lot of things. People can be depressed, or manic, or hear voices, or have visual hallucinations. And you, well, I did a lot of research when this all first started happening. You don't really fit the criteria for any mental illness. You have one symptom. The voices. Mom was a bit concerned about how upset you got after your fall, and she thought you might be getting paranoid, but I think you were just really shaken up. I don't think you're paranoid. What diagnosis did the doctor give you?"

"Auditory hallucinations," Kaya said, as if reading it from a script in her head.

"That's weird," Graham said. "That's a symptom, not a diagnosis."

"Really?" Kaya asked. "Huh. Well, he asked me all sorts of questions, like if I knew what year it was, and what day, and who the president was. He asked me if I thought people on the TV or radio were talking directly to me, even though they couldn't see me. He asked if I ever went a long time without sleeping, and felt like I didn't need to sleep, or if I felt really powerful, like I could do things other people couldn't do. There were more questions, but I can't remember them. All of my answers were no."

"Yeah," Graham said. "I have to do more research. I can skip intro to psychology class in college since I took AP Psych in high school. I know most schools offer an Abnormal Psych class. I'll take it if I can."

"Abnormal," Kaya repeated softly. She looked up and watched her teammates practice without her. She started to move her head to the music, and Graham could see her mouth words to the cheers, tapping her good foot.

"You'll be back out there in a few weeks."

"I know," Kaya said. "But by then, there'll only be one game left in the season. I'm missing so much." She sighed. "I guess that's what I get for throwing myself off of the pyramid during a psychotic episode, huh?"

Graham felt a wave of anxiety flow through his gut. "Kaya, cut it out," he said. "No one thinks you did it on purpose. We've told you that. Even if the threat wasn't real, it felt real for you. It all felt real."

"Still not convinced," Kaya mumbled.

Graham faced her. "What?"

Kaya continued to watch the cheerleaders. "Nothing."

"No," Graham said. "You think that the voices are real."

Kaya nodded. "I do," she said. "I think that, somehow, I'm hearing things that others can't hear, but they're thoughts or something."

"You think you can read thoughts?" Graham asked.

Kaya shrugged. "I don't know," she said. "I just know that I'm not crazy. I'm not."

Graham nodded. "Okay," he said. "So if you can read minds, what number am I thinking of right now?"

Kaya squirmed in her seat. "I don't know," she said. "I can't hear *your* thoughts."

"Concentrate," Graham told her. "If you can hear thoughts, you could be able to read mine. I can't see why they'd be selective."

Kaya closed her eyes. Then she opened them. Her shoulders slumped. "I can't hear anything."

Graham nodded. He thought maybe he'd pushed her too hard. Maybe it had been a bad idea to challenge her thoughts. He watched the practice in silence for a few minutes. Then he turned back to Kaya. "I wonder where Dad is right now."

Kaya stared at him. "Dad?" she asked. "Huh. That's a weird thought. I don't know. I don't really think about him that much."

Graham's eyes went wide. "You don't? That surprises me. I think about him all the time."

Kaya shrugged. "I don't let myself think about him, I guess," she said. "It would probably drive me crazy if I did. I guess he needed something else in his life. I don't know what. But I'd rather he left than stay at home and be unhappy all the time, making everyone else miserable. He did what he had to do. It's hard to be angry at him. I mean, I do miss him, when I let myself." She paused. "Maybe that's more often than I'm willing to admit."

She started to fuss with the padding on the top of her crutch.

Graham thought about it. "But it's really hard on Mom. She hasn't even had any time to process anything. She's so busy just trying to keep us all afloat. I wish she could take some time to herself."

Kaya bit her lower lip, making Graham wonder if that gesture was genetic. "I think Mom keeps herself busy so she doesn't *have* to think."

"Maybe," Graham said. He looked down at the basketball court. The girls were wrapping up their practice. He suddenly noticed someone looking at him. It was Bailey. She smiled and then waved. Graham gave a small wave back and then turned to look at Kaya.

"I guess. I think all of us are dealing with his leaving differently. Mom's worrying and staying busy, I'm focusing on you and my schoolwork, and you . . ."

"What about me?" Kaya said, challenging him. "What is it I'm doing, Graham? Manufacturing voices in my head because Dad left us to find himself?"

Graham shrugged. "It has occurred to me," he said. "It all started soon after he left, right? I know you said that you try not to think about it, but you and Dad have always been close, closer than I ever was with him. You did a lot of stuff together. When you decided to go out for cheerleading, he was the one who went out and bought you the practice pompoms and the cheering DVDs. He encouraged you. He was happy for you. You've always looked up to him. You can't tell me that him leaving wasn't a big loss for you."

Kaya shook her head. "Are you *trying* to make me cry? Graham, whatever's going on with me, it has nothing to do with Dad. The timing's just a coincidence. Maybe it's about cheerleading. I started cheering camp right before he left." She reached out and touched Graham's hand. "I'm not ignoring how horrible it is that Dad left," she said. "It's awful. Like I said, I do miss him. I'm just not mad at him. I know he'll be back someday. I don't think things will ever be the same. But he said he was looking for something. Maybe he'll find it. And if he doesn't, maybe he'll realize that it's just not out there. I have no doubt that if I get married someday, Dad will be there to walk me down the aisle."

Graham was amazed by his sister's thought process. He did have to admit, her ideas were very lucid. She did not seem like a girl who was dealing with her father's leaving in a dysfunctional way. She seemed more emotionally healthy than him and their mother in the whole matter. That actually concerned him more than if it wasn't true. If her voices had been caused by stress, there would be more of a chance that they would resolve, either over time on their own, or with the help of a good therapist. But if they were caused by a chronic illness, she would most likely have to deal with the repercussions for the rest of her life. "When's your MRI?"

Kaya sighed exaggeratedly. "Would you please stop obsessing about what caused my voices?" she begged. "Can't we just move on to something else?"

"I'm just worried, that's all," Graham said. "I don't think you have a brain tumor, of course, but it would be nice to hear it from a professional."

Kaya's face softened. "It's next Thursday," she said. "It's in the morning. Mom said I can skip school that day. But by the end of the day, I will have irrefutable evidence that I do, indeed, have a brain." She laughed. "No more jokes about having rocks in there."

Graham had to smile. "Yeah. I guess I'll have to come up with something else to tease you about!"

The next Thursday, Graham studied with Chet and their friend Chris at the school library after last period. Finals were coming up, and then school would be out for winter break. Graham had already sent out his college applications along with his SAT scores, but he still wanted to do well for the rest of the year. He wasn't in contention for valedictorian, but he didn't care—he didn't want to have to give a speech anyway—but he did want a final grade point average he could be proud of. When he got home, his mother and Kaya were there. Kaya was watching TV and eating from a large bowl of popcorn. Mrs. Reed was at the dining room table, looking at a ledger book through her reading glasses. She looked up when Graham came in and smiled.

"Hi, Graham," she said. "How was your day?"

Graham threw his backpack on a chair and took off his jacket.

"Uneventful," he said. "Everyone's just getting ready for exams and Christmas. How did the MRI go?"

Kaya looked up at Graham briefly and then looked back at the TV, stuffing popcorn into her mouth.

"It went fine," Mrs. Reed said. "We went early in the day. Dr. Creston called this afternoon after viewing the results. Basically, most everything looked normal."

She clicked the top of her pen over and over.

"There was some indication of a slight enlargement, like a bony protrusion, in the receptive language area of her brain that could be indicative of auditory hallucinations, but Kaya said she wasn't hearing any voices at the time of the test. Dr. Creston said it was unusual, but not impossible. He said there's no reason to be concerned. He's going to study it more. He thinks it could be a genetic thing. You know, some sort of evolutionary thing that most people got rid of over the centuries but some people retained. It's possible you and I could have it too. He really didn't think we needed to worry. But for sure, there are no brain tumors."

Kaya looked up again. "And no rocks."

Graham smiled. Then his smile fell away as he looked at his mother. "So what do we do now?"

Mrs. Reed shrugged. "Kaya keeps taking the medication, and we watch her. We make sure there aren't other incidents. And if there aren't any, we know that the meds are working. If there are, we try a different medication."

Graham shook his head. "It's like we're shooting darts at the voices," he said, "and hoping they stick where we want them."

"That's kind of what Dr. Creston said," Mrs. Reed said. "He said that everyone's brain chemistry is different, so we don't have any definite idea of what will work. He said that if this ran in the family, we could look at what medications worked and what didn't, but we don't have that luxury. Not that I'm complaining."

Graham nodded. "So are you gonna let Kaya continue with cheer?"

"I'm not quitting cheerleading," Kaya said without lifting her gaze from the TV. "You can't make me."

Mrs. Reed closed her eyes and then opened them. "I'm not gonna stop her from having the life she wants," she said. "No one at school knows about any of this. We'll just keep it between the three of us, okay? It's not that it's anything to be ashamed of, but there is a stigma. I don't want Kaya to have to deal with that at her age."

"I agree," Graham said. "So for now, we just go on like nothing's happening."

"Away from home," Mrs. Reed corrected. "We're not trying to convince ourselves that it's not happening, Graham. We're just not broadcasting it."

"Okay," Graham said. He walked into the kitchen and looked in the refrigerator. He stared at shelves full of food but found nothing he wanted. He closed the door and went to the fruit bowl on the counter. He grabbed an apple and took a big bite before sitting down at the kitchen table to chew.

So now they had some answers. Kaya didn't have a brain tumor, and he was glad. But the answers they had were not satisfying. The only satisfying answers would have been some indicating an easy fix. A magic pill. A small, outpatient procedure that would put everything back to normal.

Normal. Nothing felt normal. He thought back to a year ago, to a night when all four of them—he, his father, his mother, and Kaya—were sitting at the kitchen table together eating ice cream and laughing. It was Kaya's birthday. They were having ice cream for lunch at her request. Their father was telling funny stories about Kaya when she was little. Kaya was blushing, but she also had a wide smile. She loved her father. She was his favorite. Graham didn't resent their relationship. Sometimes he envied it, but he knew that he was closer to their mother. They seemed like the ideal family. Now so much had changed.

He wondered if there was something amiss in the universe that had caused so much to change in so little time.

A week later, Kaya was back at cheerleading, and Graham was back in the bleachers. He watched his sister as she stood in the periphery of the group, watching, trying to get back in the groove. Two of the other girls were trying to pull her back in, one of them showing her some new steps. After some time, Kaya started to warm up, both physically and mentally, and Graham saw her start to smile and laugh with her friends. But not everyone seemed happy that Kaya was back. Jill stood off to the side, her arms folded in front of her, frowning as she watched the other girls starting to have fun with Kaya. Graham watched her with interest. Even though he knew it was impossible that Jill had conveyed messages to Kaya telling her she was going to hurt her, it seemed evident that there was no love lost between the two girls.

As practice progressed, Miss Green had Kaya stand to the side, doing the simple steps and no jumps. She sat out of the pyramid all together. Just as she had always been, Jill was relegated to the middle level as Bailey climbed up and stood proudly atop her back. Kaya stood with Miss Green and watched. It was unclear if she would be returning to the pyramid after what had happened. She smiled up at Bailey, who smiled down at her and waved.

On the way home, Graham suggested they stop for ice cream at their favorite parlor, Pistachios. Kaya ordered a small hot fudge sundae, and Graham got a banana split.

"I saw you and Miss Green talking," Graham said. "Anything special?"

Kaya smiled. "She told me that I'd been doing a really good job with dance ideas," she said. "The team voted for Hannah for team captain next year, and she said she'd like me to assist her with coming up with some new steps for next year. Basic choreography. I'd love to do that. I can't do a whole dance, but I can make suggestions." She beamed. "Miss Green said that all the girls missed me when I was gone. She said I have great team spirit, and they really need someone like me around to help keep them motivated. Graham, I think that she thinks I can be captain one day! That would be so awesome! If I get to be captain, I might be able to get onto a cheer squad in college, especially with choreography experience."

"That's great, Ky!"

He was genuinely happy for her. It sounded like she was very popular on her team, and she had great potential. Not only that, but it appeared that no one suspected anything about her mental health issue. That would make things a lot easier for Kaya. If anyone on the team knew, they might plant doubt about her ability in the minds of the other girls. Graham ate his ice cream, still smiling.

"I hate that I'll miss seeing you cheer when I go to college next year."

Kaya gave him a sweet smile. "I'll miss you, too, Graham," she said. "It will really be different without you. And I'll have three years in high school as the only Reed kid. I wish we were closer in age, so we could have more time together."

Kaya's words made Graham feel warm inside. He was looking forward to going to college, but he dreaded leaving his family. He didn't want to leave them with so much going on. There were still several months before college would start in September. He would do everything he could to help to get things back to normal as much as he could. And if things couldn't be normal, he would help his mother and sister define a new normal. When he finally went away to school, he wanted to know that he was leaving things in very good order.

CHAPTER 6

"ARE YOU SURE THAT'S ENOUGH underwear?" Mrs. Reed asked.

Graham looked up from his packing and glared at his mother. "Mom," he said, "I think I know how much underwear is enough. I have like fourteen pairs. But you know the funny thing? They have Targets in Palmetto. I can buy more underwear if I get desperate."

Mrs. Reed sat on the edge of the bed. "Go easy on me, Graham Cracker," she said softly. "This is the first time I'm sending my child off to college. I want to make sure I do it right."

Graham instantly regretted being snarky to his mother. "I know," he said. "It's my first time going away to college, too, and my first time away from home for more than a couple of days. We're all gonna have to adjust some. But it will be okay. We're all in a good place now. And I have a cellular phone now, so I can call you whenever I want to, and you'll know that I can reach someone if there's an emergency."

"Well, at least there's that." Mrs. Reed smiled. "I remember when cellular phones came out. We called them car phones. I was in college when my father first got one. We were all so excited. He drove a few blocks away and called the house phone. My mother answered, and we all passed the phone around. Then he came home and took us all out in the car so we could call our friends." She laughed. "And now people have them in their pockets. And text messaging! Maybe I'll get one soon. I'm still getting used to using a tablet."

Graham smiled. "I'm glad my computer's still relevant," he said. "It would be awful if we had to buy a new one." He closed the box he was working on and opened his trunk. "I have to decide what I'm bringing with me besides clothes and school supplies."

He looked around his room, his eyes falling on a family picture that had been taken five years earlier on a family trip to Disney World. He glanced at his mother. She smiled and nodded. Graham grabbed the frame, wrapped it in newspaper, and put it on the bottom of his trunk.

"I wonder if he wonders where I'm going to school."

Mrs. Reed shrugged. "Maybe he still talks to his parents," she said, "but I doubt it. It's not like he left because we stopped loving each other. At least that's what he said. And I know he loves you and Kaya very much." She looked down. "I think if he was going to reach out to anyone, it would be you two. It makes me sad that he never knew about what Kaya went through this year. I know he would have wanted to help her if he could. And then I'd want to be able to tell him how great she's doing now. Not one word about hearing voices, or anything strange for six months. The medication really works, Graham. I think we got the miracle we had been hoping for."

Graham nodded. "It really has been a relief. There was a while when I was really worried about her future, but now she seems to be back to her old self again. I mean, I'm guessing she is. She's always up there in her room with her friends, giggling. I'm guessing they're talking about the boys they like and probably making up new dance steps. I just wish that Cat would stop looking at me like I'm her favorite dessert or something."

Mrs. Reed laughed. "She has a schoolgirl crush. I used to have them all the time. I thought I was being so discrete, but I must have been awful around the boys I liked, exaggerating smiles and singling them out when I walked by them standing with their friends. I probably embarrassed them.

I'm glad I didn't meet your father until after college. Any earlier, and I probably would have scared him off!"

She appeared to realize what she had said and put her hand to her mouth. "I guess it just took a few extra years for that to happen."

Graham grimaced. Sometimes things would be going along so well and then something would happen to remind them of what they had lost.

"It's been a year," he said. "We're doing great, Mom." He reached over and gave her a kiss on the cheek. "Did you mention something about baking cookies to bring with me tomorrow? I think that would make the transition much easier for me." He gave his mother a grin.

Mrs. Reed laughed. "Yes, I did mention making some pecan coconut double chocolate chip cookies for you," she said. "But I think I might need some help. Wanna take a break from packing for a minute?"

Graham nodded, pushed the cover of the trunk closed, and got up to follow his mother to the kitchen.

It was their last dinner together. Mrs. Reed made hamburgers out of ground beef and onion soup mix and placed them in buns—Graham's favorite meal. He loaded his up with lettuce, tomato, pickles, onions, ketchup, and mustard before taking his first bite. Ketchup squirted out the side of the burger and ran down his hands. Everyone laughed. That's what happened every time. Kaya spent some time arranging avocado strips on her burger patty and then writing her initials in ketchup on the bun. She put it all together and ate her burger happily. Graham had mixed feelings. It was wonderful to be eating a meal with his family, and having such an enjoyable time, but it would be the last time until Thanksgiving, and on the holiday, things would be hectic.

He watched his mother take small bites from her burger and wipe her mouth compulsively with her napkin after each one. She caught him watching and smiled as she chewed.

"I'm gonna go to Cat's house for an hour or so after dinner if that's okay," Kaya said after taking her last bite. "It will be our last chance to see each other before school starts and I have cheerleading practice." She looked at Graham. "I won't be long, I promise. We just need to talk about some things. Girls stuff, you know. When I get home, we can hang out if you want."

Graham nodded. "That's fine. Just please tell me that the girl stuff isn't about Cat wanting to go out with me."

Kaya laughed. "Graham, yeah, she liked you for a few months, but she knows you're going away. Now she's hoping to get the attention of someone closer to our age who isn't going to college. I think you're safe. At least for now. We'll see how things are by Christmas."

"Okay," Graham said. "When you get back, we can grab some of the cookies Mom and I made earlier and you can help me finish packing. I feel like I'm forgetting a ton of stuff, but I have no idea what."

"I don't know what kinds of things boys need for college," Kaya said. She giggled. "Condoms?"

"Kaya!" Mrs. Reed exclaimed, but then she laughed too. "Well, I guess you're not wrong. Better safe than sorry."

Graham felt his face get hot. He hadn't told his family that Gina Simpson was also going to State. He might go ahead and get the condoms, just in case. "Just go to Cat's house already."

After Kaya left, Graham and his mother sat at the table, talking about what Graham should expect at college.

"I remember how tempting it was to just sleep through class if I'd had a late night," Mrs. Reed said. "But you're on a scholarship, Graham. You'll need to take things seriously. If you lose the scholarship, we won't be able to pay for you to go to State. You'll have to transfer to community college, and that won't be challenging for you at all."

Graham gave his mother a reassuring smile. "Mom, I've always taken school seriously," he said. "I'm not gonna stop now. If I do decide to engage in drinking and debauchery, I'll save it all for the weekends. Plus, I don't like to stay up late. I like the mornings much better."

Mrs. Reed laughed. "You're really gonna have to find other morning people when you get there," she said. "There may have been morning people in my dorm, but I never met them. I was too busy sleeping and staying up late!"

Graham smiled. "Is there anything you want me to do to help you out before we go tomorrow? This is your last chance."

Mrs. Reed thought about it. "Garbage day is Tuesday this week because of Labor Day," she said. "I can bring out the cans on Monday night, but would you mind collecting the garbage and putting it outside so all I have to do is drag it out?"

Graham nodded. "That's easy enough. I thought you'd probably ask me to go out and clean out the gutters before it gets dark out or something. So the kitchen, both bathrooms, and the bedrooms?"

Mrs. Reed nodded. "Kaya may have already emptied her wastebasket," she said. "She usually takes care of it herself. But why don't you check it anyway? That way she doesn't have to worry about it when we get home from Palmetto. Thanks so much for offering to help me out, Graham. I'm really gonna miss having another set of responsible hands around here. It was much easier . . ." She trailed off.

Graham sighed. "I know." He looked at the floor. "I'm still mad at him for not even acknowledging my graduation. A card would have been nice."

Mrs. Reed nodded. "I just hope he's okay," she said quietly. "I can sit here and be mad at him for not contacting us, but what if it's because something's wrong?" She leaned closer. "I have to admit, Graham, that ever since things started happening with Kaya this year, I've wondered if maybe something wasn't going on with your father, you know, mental-health wise."

Graham raised his brows. "Really?" he asked. "That never even occurred to me."

"Yes," Mrs. Reed said. "There's a strong genetic component to mental illness. I learned a lot about it in the support group I went to back in February. A lot of the families have multiple members with mental health issues. Your father leaving was a shock to all of us. No one thought that anything was wrong at all. But suddenly, there it was. But when I look back, I wonder if there were signs."

"Can you think of any?" Graham asked.

Mrs. Reed stared at the wall. "The only thing I can think of is that sometimes he got really quiet, just out of the blue. I'd ask him if everything was okay, and he'd just smile and say everything was fine, he was just thinking about something at work, or something like that. Do you think it's possible he might have heard voices, too?"

Graham shook his head. "I have no idea. We didn't know that Kaya was hearing them until she said something. I guess anything's possible."

Mrs. Reed sighed deeply. "I guess it's food for thought." She smiled. "Go do the garbage," she said. "I'll take care of the dishes."

Graham went to the kitchen to get a garbage bag. He started by emptying the bathroom trash, and then moving on to the bedrooms. He would save the kitchen trash for last. He made his way to Kaya's room and opened the door. He felt strange walking into her room when she wasn't there. It felt like he was invading her private sanctum. He looked around. Everything looked neat and orderly, and the bed was made. The only signs that the room was inhabited by a teenage girl were the pajamas strewn over the bed and CDs sprawled out on the desk. There were also shoes that looked to have been kicked haphazardly around the floor at the end of the day. He found her wastebasket under her desk. He reached for it, dumped the contents into the bag, and put it back down when something caught his eye at the bottom, something colorful. He looked closer, and then reached down to pluck it up with his fingers. He brought it closer to his face. It was a capsule, some sort of medication. Kaya only took one medication, the antipsychotic she had been on for six months to help suppress the voices. A thought struck him.

He put the capsule down on the desk and looked into the garbage bag. He couldn't see anything on top, so he started to rifle through the contents. It didn't take him long to find what he was looking for. A capsule. Then another. And another. By the time he was done searching, he had found five capsules. Almost a week's worth of medication. He put them in his pocket.

Graham sat on Kaya's bed, a feeling of despair coming over him. Every day, Mrs. Reed gave Kaya her medication at breakfast time, watching her put the capsule in her mouth and take a drink of orange juice. But somehow, all of these pills were in Kaya's garbage. Somehow, Kaya was not swallowing the capsules. She must have been spitting them out and throwing them away later. Maybe that was the reason that Kaya had been emptying her own garbage, so that her mother and brother wouldn't see the evidence in the trash. He wondered how long she had been doing that. Kaya seemed to be doing so well for the past six months. She never talked about hearing voices anymore, and she seemed happy. So maybe this was a recent thing, maybe just this week. If that was the case, Graham worried that the voices would slowly creep back into Kaya's daily life, and she would become distressed again. But if it had been longer than a week, at least a month, or more, that would mean that even without the medication, Kaya was doing all right. In a way, Graham hoped that was the case. He would be so happy if the voices had somehow gone away on their own and Kaya didn't need to take the medication, especially with him leaving for college. He wouldn't be there to keep an eye on her all the time, or to watch cheerleading practice to make sure she was safe. For now, he had to go find the medication bottle, to confirm that these capsules were indeed the antipsychotic medication. He wanted to count them, to make sure that these weren't just some extra pills that Kaya had somehow come upon and thrown away. He had to be sure, before he confronted her. Because he was going to confront her as soon as she came home. He couldn't leave the next day without knowing what was going on.

After he put out the garbage, Graham left his mother in the living room watching the news on TV and went into the kitchen. He quietly took Kaya's medication out of the cabinet and opened it. He looked inside. His heart fell. It was the same medication he had found in the wastebasket. He looked at the date on the bottle and calculated how many pills should be left and then poured the remainder in his hand. He counted them. There were exactly as many capsules as there should be. That confirmed it for him. Kaya had been tossing her medications on a daily basis. He put the capsules back in the bottle and then stowed them in their place in the cabinet. Then he went back out to the living room to watch TV with his mother.

Kaya came home forty-five minutes later. She was in a good mood. "Cat has a crush on Steve Winsor," she told her mother and brother. "She has our old middle school yearbook, and she drew a big heart around his picture! It's a really bad picture. His eyes are half closed." She laughed and sat down next to her mother.

Mrs. Reed laughed. "That's so cute," she said. Her eyes twinkled. "What about you? Do you have a crush?"

Kaya blushed. "I don't know if I have a crush," she said softly. "But there is this boy . . ."

"I knew it!" Mrs. Reed said with a smile. "What's his name?"

"Jeffrey Cohen," Kaya said. Then she closed her eyes and lifted her shoulders as if bracing herself for the reaction.

"Jeff Cohen!" Mrs. Reed exclaimed. "Oh my goodness! Kaya! You've known him since kindergarten! I remember you telling me how gross he was! This is great! I'll have to call Betsy and let her know you have a crush on her son!"

Kaya sobered quickly. "No!" she insisted. "You are not to say a word to his mother! Mom! I think he might be interested in me, at least in being friends. Don't ruin this for me! I knew I shouldn't have said anything. I forgot who I was talking to for a second."

She stood.

"Graham, I'm going upstairs to soak my head in a bucket of cold water so I never forget that I can't tell Mom any secrets, ever. Come up and bring those cookies you promised."

She turned and started to skip toward the stairs, humming.

Graham waited a bit before getting up. He was starting to wonder if he should even say anything to Kaya about what he found. She was in such a good mood. He didn't want to ruin it, especially the night before he left home. But he also needed to know if his sister was all right. He did a quick cost benefit analysis in his head and then stood. He would see how things played out before deciding what to do. He went into the kitchen and positioned several cookies on a plate, poured two glasses of milk, and put everything on a tray that his parents had gotten as a wedding gift twenty years earlier. Then he started for the stairs.

Kaya was lying on her bed, music playing from her stereo, a book held in position above her head. Graham rapped on her door softly.

"Ky, I'm ready to finish my packing."

Kaya jumped up quickly, put her book on her nightstand, and turned up the music so it could be heard in Graham's room next door.

"What CDs are you bringing?" she asked as they entered his room. She grabbed a cookie and took a large bite.

Graham rifled through his collection. "I think I'll take Nirvana, Stone

Temple Pilots, No Doubt, Beastie Boys, 311 . . . Do you ever listen to your Foo Fighters CD? Maybe I can borrow it from you."

Kaya shrugged. "You can take it. I actually have two copies. Someone gave me the second one for my fourteenth birthday." She plopped down on Graham's bed. "Your room already looks so empty."

Graham looked around. "I feel so unprepared," he admitted. "I have no idea what it will be like, being away from here. I'm a little nervous."

Kaya looked shocked. "You always seem so sure of yourself. I would think you'd be on top of it. I think it would be really fun to have my own dorm room and be able to do whatever I want, whenever I want."

"You'd probably have to still have a routine," Graham said. "Just because Mom's not around doesn't mean I can just go nuts, and not do what I have to. I still have to be responsible. You will, too, when you go away." He cleared his throat. "Like, Mom won't be there to give you your pills every day. You'll have to remember to take them yourself."

Kaya looked at her lap, her face draining of blood. "Well, that won't be a problem for me," she said. She adjusted the cuff on her jeans. "I'm pretty responsible and stuff."

Graham stared at her until she looked up and noticed.

"What?" she asked defensively.

"I emptied your trash today," he said. "Mom asked me to."

Kaya's face became even more pale. "Oh," she said. "Thanks. I was gonna get to it when we got back on Sunday. You saved me the trouble."

Graham squinted at her. "Kaya . . ." he started.

Kaya snorted. "Okay, fine. So you saw something. Why don't you just ask what you want to ask already instead of playing games with me?"

Graham nodded. "Fair enough," he said. "I found a capsule. And when I looked, I found five more of them." He reached into his pocket and showed her the contents. "Kaya, what have you been doing?"

Kaya sighed. "I put the meds under my tongue when Mom gives them to me," she said. "I take a drink, and then when she turns away, I spit them into my hand."

Graham nodded slowly. "That's what I thought," he said. "How long?"

Kaya shrugged. "Five months?"

Graham gasped. "Five months! That's almost the whole time she's been giving them to you! Kaya! You can't just do things like that!"

"Why not?" Kaya asked defiantly. "I mean, I've been fine, right? I haven't had my medication for five months, and nothing's happened. Doesn't that tell you anything? I don't need it! I'm fine without it! But Mom's so adamant about me taking it. I couldn't just tell her that I didn't want to take it anymore. And besides, it didn't do anything."

"What do you mean?" Graham asked, worried about what the answer would reveal.

Kaya shrugged again. "Bailey still hummed in class every day. People still said weird things. Sometimes I heard people saying things, and their lips weren't moving. So yeah. Nothing. But you know what? I've learned to deal with it. It doesn't bother me anymore. It's just not a problem! Graham, please don't say anything to Mom. I promise you, if it starts to become a problem, I'll just start swallowing the pills again, and Mom won't ever know the difference. I don't want to take the pills. They made me feel weird. Sometimes, my hands and feet felt strange. I can't even describe it. But it stopped as soon as I stopped taking them. I can't go back on them!"

Graham felt trapped. Kaya was putting him in a horrible position. Their mother and the doctor knew what was best for Kaya, but Kaya knew her own body, her own mind. And he was her brother. He couldn't betray her. Finally, he nodded.

"Fine," he said. "But you have to promise me that you'll talk to me on the phone every week and be honest about how things are going. I mean really honest. If I feel that you're not being honest, I'll tell Mom. And you have to listen to me. If I think things are getting worse based on what you tell me, I'm gonna tell you to start taking the meds again. Do we have a deal?"

Kaya thought about it for a moment and then nodded. She stuck out her hand. "Deal," she said. They shook hands firmly. "Let's talk about something else now, okay? I have a few more ideas about what CDs you need to bring that won't make you look like a total loser to the other guys on your floor. " She sorted through his collection. "No boy bands. Good. So you take Bush, Green Day, Matchbox Twenty . . . oh, man! When did you get this Savage Garden CD? You need to leave this for me!"

Kaya: Sophomore Year

KAYA WAS HAPPY TO BE back at school for sophomore year, and especially to be back at cheer practice. After her accident the year before, she'd had to sit out and watch, and now she would be able to participate fully in the team activity. She ran into Bailey during first period class, and they clasped hands and smiled at each other.

"I can't wait for practice today," Kaya said. "Do you think we'll still do the pyramid, or do you think Miss Green will give it to the younger girls after tryouts?"

Bailey shrugged. "I'd be okay with not doing it this year," she said. "It's hard having someone standing on your back like that. It's cool to be up there. I know Jill hates it, too." She leaned in closer. "She always talked about wanting to be on top. She was pretty pissed off when I got your spot after your accident."

"It wasn't my fault," Kaya said. Then, quietly, she added, "Maybe now she'll be more careful about knocking me over."

Bailey looked up. "What?"

Kaya smiled. "Oh, nothing." She sat at her desk. "Sit next to me. Just no singing this year, okay?"

Bailey blushed. "I stopped doing that after you told me."

Kaya laughed. "Sometimes," she said. "But sometimes, you let it slip out."

Bailey lowered her head. "Can you please throw something at me if you hear me do it again?"

Kaya nodded. "I promise. The teachers might not let you get away with it this year."

Kaya sat with Bailey and her friends Rayna and Cat at lunch. After they started to eat, a few boys from Kaya and Cat's elementary school approached the table. Jeff Cohen was among them.

"Hey, Kaya and Cat, can we sit here?" Jeff asked.

Kaya smiled. "Sure," she said. When the boys sat down, Kaya introduced them all. "You guys know Cat, and this is Rayna and Bailey. Bailey does cheer with me. I met Rayna last year in English class. Guys, this is Jeff, Greg, and Taylor."

Everyone said hi, and conversation ensued. Kaya was excited about having the boys sit with them. It felt like they were all finally growing up, maturing. Maybe Jeff had decided to sit there so he could be near Kaya. The thought made her slightly giddy. It was hard to tell, though, because Jeff spoke to each girl equally.

The six of them sat together every day, and Kaya still couldn't tell if Jeff was interested. She would watch during lunch as he looked around at everyone he spoke to, to see if he paid special attention to her. If anything, he tended to talk the most to Rayna. They had a lot in common. Both of them were Jewish and went to the same temple. Jeff's grandparents lived in Garrison, and so did Rayna's. Kaya couldn't think of anything she had in common with Jeff except the fact that they had gone to the same elementary school.

It was the third week of school, and Kaya got to the cafeteria after Jeff. She saw the seat open next to him and took advantage of the situation. She sat down and turned to look at him. "What's up?" she asked in a friendly manner.

Jeff smiled. "Not much. We have a test in Spanish after lunch. I'm not sure I know all of my conjugations. I need to get at least a B."

"I wish I could help you," Kaya said. "But I take French. And I'm not the best at it, either."

Rayna sat down across from Jeff. "What are you guys talking about?"

"Spanish," Jeff said. "I have a test. I'm worried about some verb conjugation."

Rayna smiled. "I can help you with that. I'm in honors Spanish. I've got the conjugations down. What are you struggling with?"

Kaya shifted in her seat. Her foot was up against the leg of the table. She was sitting in the awkward seat that everyone always avoided due to lack of space. She shuffled her feet and accidently kicked Jeff.

"I want to jump over the table and touch you," Jeff said.

Kaya turned quickly to look at Jeff, who was looking at . . . Rayna.

She felt her body stiffen.

Rayna was going over the conjugation of the Spanish verb estar. "Estoy, estás, está . . ."

"I want to kiss you," Jeff said. "I want to put my tongue in your mouth. I wonder if it's soft. I wonder if you'd let me touch your boobs."

Kaya gasped. Rayna looked over at her. "What's wrong, Kaya?"

Kaya quickly concluded that what she had heard had been one of her voices. No way would Jeff have said those things to Rayna. Rayna would have been horrified! She wouldn't still be helping him prepare for his test.

Kaya shook her head. She pushed her chair back. "Nothing's wrong," she said. "I just remembered that I have something to do for history class next period. I have to go get something from my locker."

She stood up and grabbed her tray.

"I'll just take my sandwich with me." She said goodbye to her friends, pushed her chair in, and headed for the tray return.

Once she left the cafeteria, she stood against a wall and closed her eyes. This was the first time in a long time that she had heard anything quite so vividly. It was as if Jeff had been talking right to her, about her friend, as if it were okay to say things like that. No, Jeff wouldn't have done that.

Kaya felt funny. She felt like she was missing something. She wasn't quite sure what it was, but suddenly, she knew nothing was ever going to happen between her and Jeff.

There had never been any indication that Jeff liked her, but now she was convinced that Jeff liked Rayna, even if it was just from what she had heard in her head.

The next day, she made a point of not sitting next to Jeff, and she decided that she would do the same every day forward.

Chapter 7

GRAHAM TOOK TO COLLEGE LIKE a fish to water. For the first time in his life, he felt surrounded by people who were just like him; they wanted to learn and prepare for the life they wanted. Not everyone was like that. Like his mother had told him, many students were more interested in the nightlife the freedom from their parents brought them, and they stayed out until all hours of night, coming home drunk. Graham's roommate started his college career in that manner, and Graham was nervous that their relationship would end up adversarial, but after about two weeks of hangovers on Sunday mornings, Tyler decided he'd had enough. Then he and Graham became friends.

Neither of them were interested in joining a fraternity. Not only did they want to be able to choose their own friends, but they also didn't have the money to pay the associated joining fees. But they found other things they enjoyed doing. They very quickly found the arcade in the student center and made some friends there. Graham joined a chess club, and Tyler went for a hiking group. They both enjoyed going to concerts and movies on campus. Graham found time to have lunch with Gina Simpson, who was struggling to find her own group of friends and welcomed the company. They talked about their time at Wisteria High, and their memories of school.

"I remember you back in elementary school," she told him on a cold afternoon in October as they sat in Gina's dining hall drinking coffee after their meal. "You were so serious. No one ever really cared about those spelling bees Mr. Fine always made us do in fifth grade, but you were always totally prepared." She laughed. "But then Courtney Jefferson would beat you at the last minute. I wonder what ever happened to her."

"She moved to Clemens in eighth grade," Graham said. "She got to spend the next several years tormenting her peers in a new school."

Gina smiled. "I think she liked you," she said. "She wanted you to see how smart she was. But I think it backfired on her. Do you not like smart girls, Graham?" Her grin was teasing.

Graham smiled. "No, I like smart girls. I just wanted to win! And she kept me from winning!" He paused. "You think she liked me? God, I was clueless. But I wasn't really interested in girls back in fifth grade anyway."

"Oh yeah?" Gina asked, leaning a bit closer. "When did you start getting interested in girls?"

Graham concentrated on not blushing. "I don't know, maybe sixth grade?" He laughed. "Not one girl in particular. That came later."

"And who was the first girl that caught your attention?"

Graham could tell that Gina was flirting with him, and he was both elated and terrified. "Joanna Durst," he said. "She broke my heart when she started dating Kevin Forman."

"They're still together," Gina said. Then she tilted her head. "And who was the last girl that caught your attention?"

Now Graham had no control over the reddening of his face. "Do I really have to tell you?" he asked, smiling weakly.

Gina laughed. "No, you don't. But maybe if you told her how you felt, she would tell you she felt the same way, and then you wouldn't have to wonder."

Graham felt his vocal chords freeze. He took a sip of his coffee and cleared his throat. "But she could also say that she doesn't feel the same way, and then that would suck."

Gina shook her head. "Maybe," she said. "But maybe not. Sometimes you have to take a chance in life." She took a sip of her coffee, gazing at him over the rim. "C'mon, Graham, I'm pretty sure we're on the same page here."

Graham let his shoulders relax a bit. "Okay," he said. "It's Mandy Connor." He watched Gina's expression change to one of horror and he laughed. "I'm just kidding Gina. It's you. Of course it's you. I've, uh, been interested in you since the beginning of senior year. I was just too much of a wimp to ever say anything."

Gina's smile returned. "You're not the only wimp," she said. "I've actually been, uh, interested in you since junior year." It was her turn to blush. "See, that wasn't so bad. We both said it. Now we don't have to say it again."

Graham felt a new warmth inside him that didn't come from the coffee. "My sister guessed last year that I liked you. I told her she was crazy, but she was actually right."

"I remember your sister," Gina said. "I wasn't at that basketball game last year when she fell, but I heard you were. That must have been horrible."

Graham nodded "It was probably the most horrifying thing I've ever been through. For a minute, I worried that she had fallen on her head and was dead. I never ran so fast in my life to get to her. When I saw that she was conscious and moving around, I was so relieved."

"Did she say what happened?" Gina asked. "What made her fall?"

"Uh," Graham started. "She lost her balance. It was weird, because she had done the pyramid all season, but that day, she was just off."

Gina nodded. "Laila Parks was at the game," she said. "She said that Kaya shouted out 'no' before she fell, like yelled it. She said she sounded angry." Gina moved even closer to Graham. "I also heard rumors that Kaya said one of the girls knocked her off on purpose, but she didn't say who."

Graham stared at Gina. "I hadn't heard that," he said carefully. "By the time I got there, we were just concentrating on getting her to the hospital." Graham felt bad lying to Gina, especially after finally admitting how he felt about her. "And she's never said anything like that to me or our mother."

Gina nodded. "Sometimes people have to make things up if they don't know what really happened. She seemed fine when she got back to cheering, though, but I bet she'll never get back on the top of a pyramid!" She laughed.

Graham smiled. "You've never met my sister. She's probably got them making a taller pyramid this year." He let some time pass by drinking more of his coffee. "So, you know, we just admitted that we're, like, interested in each other, Gina. Maybe we should do more than just have lunch every now and then. There are other meals. Dinner, for instance."

Gina nodded. "I, for one, am a big fan of dinner."

"Me, too," he said. "Unfortunately, I'm also an unemployed freshman on a scholarship, so I can't ask you out to a formal restaurant. But I do hear they're having fried chicken at my dining hall on Friday night, if you'd like to bring your meal card and join me."

Gina laughed. "I love fried chicken," she said. "Should I dress for the occasion?"

"Dress code is jeans and a sweater," Graham said, "but they do accept corduroys and sweats, as well."

The weekly calls with Kaya were going well. She had not been having any particularly bad voices and reported that what she did hear, she tolerated.

"People say things about the food in the cafeteria," she said. "But it's not anything I haven't heard before. They say it sucks. Bailey still hums in class, and sometimes she sings, but she stops when I tell her to. Mr. Briggs brushed by me in the hall the other day and said he only has two thousand one hundred and twelve days until he can retire. But enough about me. How was your date with Gina?"

Graham smiled. "Things are going great. I was actually able to take her out to McDonald's this week, and then to a free campus movie. She said she's gonna treat this week. I think maybe KFC and the arcade."

"No one can top the two of you for fancy and romantic date ideas," Kaya said.

Graham could picture her rolling her eyes.

"What about Jeff?" Graham asked. "Has anything happened with him?"

Kaya was silent for a moment. Then she spoke. "I'm not sure about Jeff. I don't really think he's all that into me."

Graham had the old familiar feeling he got when he knew he was going to hear something he didn't want to hear. "Why is that?" he ventured.

"I don't know," she said. "It's a feeling."

Graham sighed. "It was a voice, wasn't it?"

"Sometimes, I think the voices tell me things that I might have already figured out on my own," Kaya said flatly. "But yes. We were sitting next to each other at lunch last month, in a group of our friends. Rayna came over to the table, and I heard Jeff, well, have some thoughts about her that I'd rather not repeat."

Graham slumped over a bit. "Kaya—"

"No, don't say anything, okay? Maybe I knew it already. I probably saw him looking at her in a certain way. Since I heard that, I've been watching, and they do seem to look at each other a lot. But I haven't heard him say anything else about her. Obviously, I'm not sitting next to him anymore. Probably by next week, he'll be sitting next to Rayna."

"I'm sorry, Kaya," Graham said honestly. "But maybe it's for the best. You need to be with someone who looks at you that way, not your friend." He paused. "Do you think you might need to—"

"No," Kaya said quickly. "Everything's okay. I'm doing fine. No one's trying to hurt me, I'm not delusional or paranoid or anything. I'm not gonna take the meds, Graham. But thanks for checking. Listen, I have to go. I'm meeting up with Bailey to practice. Oh, I didn't tell you the biggest thing! Jill got kicked off the cheerleading team!"

Graham's eyes widened. "Really? Why?"

"She got caught doing that thing she wanted to do to me last year, you know, with the milk and the laxatives, only she tried to do it with Bailey's water bottle. Miss Green came into the locker room and found her with the evidence! Jill got all defensive, but then started to cry when she realized she had been caught red-handed! Anyway, Miss Green was really pissed off. But I'm glad she's gone. I never trusted her. I've refused to do any complicated or tricky things with her as far as cheering, and now, no one else would want to. It does throw off our numbers a bit, but that's okay. Miss Green fills in sometimes during practice if someone's out sick or something. She's so much fun. I wish I could be friends with her, but she's a teacher. Maybe someday when I'm older I'll look her up."

"I'm glad you like her so much," Graham said. "It's nice to have a teacher in your corner. Maybe someday she can write you a college recommendation letter. It would probably be really nice. Listen, go practice with Bailey. I have to work on a research paper that's due at the end of the semester."

Kaya laughed. "You're such a nerd, Graham," she said. "It's not even Halloween yet, and you're already working on your term paper. You've still got two months! Procrastinate a little! Call Gina or something. The paper will still be there!"

Graham snickered. "You do you, Kaya, and I'll do me. We'll both be fine. I'll talk to you next week. Tell Mom I'll call her tomorrow. I love you. Bye."

"Bye. Love you."

After Graham got off the phone, he looked at his pile of library books for his paper and his notes strewn across his desk. Suddenly, it all seemed too much. He sat on his bed and pulled his cell phone from his pocket.

"Hey, Gina," he said when she answered, "what are you up to right now?"

He met her in the lobby of her dorm. She was wearing a heavy jacket and a ski cap.

"It's so cold out today," she said. "When I came back from my last class, it was windy. It's not even November yet, Graham. What's it gonna be like in January? Did we both make huge mistakes not applying to schools in Florida?"

Graham laughed. "It is really cold. I definitely need to get a heavier jacket when I go home for Thanksgiving. We're only three hours from home. Wouldn't think it would be so different here. I guess it must be due to the lake or something."

Gina shivered. "I'm already feeling it just when someone opens the door."

Graham looked at her with sympathy. "Do you just want to go up to your room and hang out there? That way you don't have to go out at all. Maybe we can get dinner at your dining hall."

A smile crossed Gina's face. "Are you sure?" she asked. "That doesn't sound like the most exciting date."

Graham smiled. "I just saw relief all over your face when I suggested it. You don't have to worry about me, Gina. I'm fine hanging out in your room. You have a VCR, right? We can sit on your bed and watch a movie. We can grab some hot chocolate pouches from the dining hall before we go up and heat up some water in your hot pot. C'mon, it will be fun." He grabbed her gloved hand. "And you won't need these arctic-level gloves to keep your hands warm."

They worked their way back to the elevator and to Gina's room on the third floor.

Before they went inside, Gina turned to Graham. "Dana's here. So maybe I should get this done now." She reached up and kissed Graham. "Hi, Graham," she said softly.

Graham smiled at her. Then she reached over and kissed her back. "Hey there, Gina." He put his arms around her and embraced her. They stood that way for about thirty seconds and then let their arms fall before Gina opened the door.

"Hey, you guys," Dana said, looking up from her book. "Too cold for you out there?"

"Yeah," Graham said, sitting on Gina's bed. "I think I might have seen a snowman running for shelter in the sauna."

Dana laughed. "I'm going to a meeting at my sorority in a while, and if I don't show up, I'll get in trouble. I guess I'll brave the tundra. What are you two up to?"

Gina was sorting through her video tapes. "I have *Jack Frost* with Michal Keaton," she said, and then she laughed. "Maybe not. We're just gonna watch a movie. You can watch with us until you have to go if you want."

They ended up putting on *Halloweentown*, one of Gina's favorite movies. "Halloween is only a week away," she said. "I hope it's not so cold that we can't go to a party. I really want to dress up and go out. It's our first year in college. I won't let the weather stop me." She gasped with delight. "We should do a couple's costume!"

Graham froze, and Dana rolled her eyes. "That would be the perfect way to get yourself laughed out of a party."

Graham smiled at Gina. "I'll do whatever you want me to," he said, reaching over to kiss her.

Gina tilted her head. "Well, maybe not a couple's costume, but more like something similar. Maybe something that just the two of us know is matching."

The movie started, and Graham leaned back against the wall, his arm around Gina's shoulder. Dana sat on the floor.

When the movie ended, Gina sat contented on the bed, a lazy smile on her face. "I feel so good every time I see that," she said. "But we do have to come up with costume ideas."

Dana stood. "I have to go, you guys," she said. "I'm already gonna be late. Have fun deciding. And by the way, I will *not* participate in a three-way costume, or any other three-way for that matter, so don't even think about it." She put on her jacket, scarf, hat, and gloves, said goodbye, and left.

"How about something from *Scream*?" Graham recommended.

Gina shook her head. "No horror. I hate horror. It gives me nightmares." Her eyes brightened. "What about Cartman and Kenny from *South Park*? That would be awesome! We could wear coats and hats, and not have to worry about being freezing!"

"But if we go to a party, it might get hot with all the people," Graham warned. "And if we took off our coats, we would be out of costume."

"Oh, right." Gina contemplated. "I'm guessing you wouldn't be into Raggedy Ann and Andy." Graham shook his head. "I figured. Gumby and Pokey? The guys from Kiss? Superheroes?"

Graham grinned and reached toward Gina's body. "I'd love to see you as Wonder Woman," he said, nuzzling his face against her shoulder. "A little leotard, some cleavage, and you can't forget her magic Lasso of Truth."

Gina smiled and fell into Graham's embrace on the bed. They let themselves slide down onto the mattress, entwined in each other's arms. "And if I had Wonder Woman's lasso right now," Gina said softly, "what truth would you be telling me?"

Graham laughed, leaning in close to whisper in Gina's ear. Then he pulled away and looked into her eyes. Her brows were lifted in surprise. Graham's smile slowly straightened out, and he gently bridged the distance between his lips and hers. They continued to kiss for a while before they moved on to the next step.

"When is Dana coming back?" he asked.

"I think we have some time," Gina said, staring into his eyes above her.

"Time for what?" he teased.

"Well, I know what *I* want to do. The question is, what do *you* want to do?"

"I think I might want to see if you'll still be cold if I take off all of your clothes."

Gina smiled. "I wasn't really that cold. I just wanted an excuse to get you up here while my roommate was gone." She reached up to kiss him, and Graham slowly lowered himself on top of her.

About half an hour later, they were lying together, cuddled up under the covers. They were both quiet, lost in their own thoughts.

Finally Graham spoke. "If I had the Lasso of Truth right now," he said gently, "what would you tell me?"

Gina looked at him, affection clear on her face. "I would tell you that I didn't know what to expect. I would tell you that I was scared, but I didn't need to be. You were perfect. That was wonderful, Graham. I couldn't have asked for a better first time."

Graham felt himself glowing, and not just from perspiration. He smiled. "That makes me so happy, Gina. I feel the same way. I always wondered who it would be, but for a long time, I've hoped it would be you, and it was. That's a dream come true." He kissed the top of her head. "I hope this is something we can do again and again."

"Me too," Gina said. She turned onto her side, facing him. "Sometimes, I wish that I could read people's minds, you know? It seems like it would make things so much easier. If I could have read your mind, I would have known last year how you felt about me, and I would have said something to you to let you know I liked you too. Maybe on some level I did know, which is what kept me going. But yeah, knowing what other people are thinking would make life simple."

Graham ran his hand through her hair. "It would be nice sometimes. But I think the anticipation is worth a lot. Besides, there's always the risk that you weren't reading minds, but you were really hearing voices."

This was the first time he had brought up this concept in front of Gina.

"And people would think you were crazy."

Gina shrugged. "Well, I just thought if I had a magic lasso, that I could also be psychic. It would be some nice superpowers. But you're right. It would be hard to differentiate what you hear with your ears and what you hear with your power. It would be really confusing."

Graham nodded. "Exactly," he said, thinking that was what often happened to Kaya. And then, as if struck by lightning, a thought came to his mind.

Kaya had told him that Jill had been kicked off the cheerleading team for trying to spike Bailey's water with a laxative. Jill had wanted to do exactly that to Kaya last year. But when Kaya had told him that she had heard Jill's plans to do so, it was during one of her auditory hallucinations. She had been on the pyramid with other team members. Penny told Kaya that Jill hadn't said anything at all. So how did Kaya know about Jill's plan? Was it possible that she had heard Jill say it some other time? But if Jill had said it out loud another time, she would have been talking to someone else, who was either involved in her scheme or would have warned Kaya. Something was off here. Something didn't make sense.

Graham decided that this wasn't the right time to think about this. He was in bed with the woman he was falling in love with, and they had just made love for the first time. He inched even closer to Gina's body and started to kiss her again. Then all other thoughts flew out of his head.

CHAPTER 8

Kaya: Junior Year

"IT'S GOOD TO HEAR FROM you," Kaya said over the phone. Since she had started her junior year in high school, her voice sounded more mature, even more confident. "It's been a few weeks. I tried to call you last week, but you weren't home."

"Was everything okay?" Graham asked, the old familiar worry coming back into his body.

"No, everything's fine," Kaya said. "I'm—I just wanted to check on you."

"You could have called my cell phone," Graham pointed out.

"I did try your cell," Kaya said. "But you haven't set up your voicemail so I couldn't leave a message."

Graham conceded that point. "I know. I have to figure out how to do that. I'm sorry I haven't called. I've just been really busy."

"With Gina?" Kaya asked. Graham could hear the laughter in her voice.

"Fine. With Gina," Graham said. "She had this thing . . ."

"I don't want to hear about Gina's thing."

"Very funny," Graham said. "No, she had a presentation, and I helped her get it ready and then stayed to watch. She got an A, so that was good."

"You two are a cute couple."

"We are," Graham said. "Any cuteness in your life these days?"

"No." She sighed. "I just haven't found Mr. Right yet. Which I guess is okay since I'm only sixteen. But there is a new teacher at Wisteria named Mr. Wright. But he's really Mr. Wrong. Plus, he's like forty and married."

Graham laughed. "How's cheerleading going?"

"We're starting to talk about who's gonna be captain for senior year." She paused. "I think I'm gonna win, Graham. It's what I've been waiting for the last three years! If I get to be captain, I get to do most of the choreography. I mean, there are certain rules and stuff, but I have a lot of leeway. I think if I become captain, I'll make Bailey my co-captain. She's really good, and she's a good team member. Did you know that she had a crush on you for, like, a couple of weeks when we were freshmen?"

"Really?" Graham remembered the one time during practice when Bailey smiled and waved at him. "I guess I'm not surprised. She was really cute back then. But I already had it bad for Gina."

"I know," Kaya said. "Remember? I knew before you did."

"No, I knew," Graham said.

"Have you decided if the two of you will live together next year when you're juniors?"

"I'd like to," Graham said. "She's gonna talk to her parents about it. We have to figure out the financial part of it all."

"Yeah, that's tricky," Kaya agreed. "You know I'll probably end up going to State, too, right? I'm hoping for an athletic scholarship."

"They have cheerleading scholarships?"

"They do," Kaya said, "and Miss Green already said she'd support me. She's getting good videos of me now so I'll have a portfolio. I have to keep getting good grades, too, though. And I'll have to audition."

"I hope you get it," Graham said. "It would be great to have you here." He secretly thought that it would be good to have Kaya nearby so he could keep a closer eye on her.

"You just want me near you so you can keep an eye on me," Kaya said intuitively.

Graham laughed. "Are you reading minds now, too?"

Kaya paused. "Too?"

Graham put his hand to his mouth. "Ky, I didn't mean anything by that."

"Sure, Graham." She hummed for a moment. "So I'm crazy in more ways than one."

"Or you're clairvoyant," Graham teased.

Kaya laughed. "Okay, I managed to stay mad at you for five seconds this time. New record. But really, Graham. Nothing's changed."

"Is Bailey still humming?"

"I haven't heard her hum for a long time."

"Have you ever asked her about the humming?"

"No." Kaya paused. "Not for a long time. Do you think I should? She doesn't think she does it anymore."

"I've been learning a lot more about this stuff," Graham said. "Auditory hallucinations usually have a negative content. And sometimes, they give people commands. Have you ever had those?"

"Are you studying me for a term paper?"

"Maybe," Graham said. "If what you say is interesting enough."

"No," Kaya said. "The voices never tell me to do anything. It's almost like it's a commentary. What else did you learn?"

"Voices are often repetitive, like people have a few that they recognize. Sometimes they hear them when there are other people around, and sometimes, when they're lying in bed at night, all alone. Sometimes they're loud, and sometimes soft. They can each have a different feel to them."

"Huh," Kaya said thoughtfully. "That doesn't sound at all like my voices. Mine are never the same people. They're usually the voices of the people standing next to me. They have the personality of that person. The volume is always around the same, and I never hear them when I'm alone."

"Your voices are weird," Graham said. "It's like you don't fit into a category."

"I've always known I was unique," Kaya joked.

Graham's phone beeped. "My call waiting is going off," he said. "It's got to be Gina. Would it be okay if I take it? I promise I'll call you in a week."

"Who am I to get in the way of true love?" Kaya purred. "Love you, big bro. Talk to you soon."

Graham pushed down the plunger on the phone. "Hello?"

"Hey sexy."

"Madonna? I told you never to call me here," Graham said.

Gina laughed. "That never gets old. What are you up to?"

"I just talked to my sister," Graham said. "I need to be better about calling her. You know, I forgot to remind her that tomorrow is our father's birthday."

"Really?" Gina asked. "You still acknowledge his birthday after he's been gone over two years?"

"He's still my father," Graham said. "I guess it just gives me a chance to think about him. I'm not gonna eat cake for him or anything. We used to do that for my Uncle Jake. Every time his birthday came around, my mother would make peanut butter chocolate chip cookies. It was what my grandmother used to make him on his birthday when they were kids. I like the idea of having a special food on your birthday. What would yours be?"

Gina laughed. "Guess!"

Graham thought about it for a moment. "Chocolate cupcakes with marshmallow frosting and graham cracker crumbs sprinkled on top."

"That's not what I would have said, but it's what I'd say now!"

Graham laughed. "That's what I'll make you next month. We'll be home for Christmas break by then and we'll have no work to do. I might have to have my mom help."

"What's yours?" Gina asked.

"Well, you know I like mint chocolate chip ice cream," he said. "So I guess mint chocolate chip ice cream."

"How should I give it to you?" Gina asked. "A cone? A bowl?"

"A bowl," Graham decided. "And maybe some chocolate sauce poured over it."

"Whipped cream?"

"Yes, and on my ice cream, too."

Gina laughed again. "You sound like a guy that needs a little loving," she said. "Do you want to come over? I've got the place to myself tonight. All night. And I'm cold and lonely."

Graham smiled. "Have I told you lately that I love you?"

"Yes," Gina said confidently. "You told me this morning. You can tell me again in just a bit. And stop on the way for whipped cream."

Graham walked into his Abnormal Psych class and took a seat close to the front. He did that deliberately so that if the professor looked out, he would notice him awake and alert and not dozing off like some of the students who sat in the back. This was the most important class he had. It was the only one that really applied to him, at least in the first two years of school. He paid close attention and did all the assigned readings. He was learning about the symptoms, causes, and treatments of mental illness, as well as some information about medications, too, but he would have to take a Psychopharmacology class to learn more. To get into that class, he would need to take an Intro to Chemistry class. After he was done with all of that, he might as well major in psych. He figured he would have a lot of credits toward it already. Plus, he enjoyed learning about the subject. He just didn't know if he wanted to be a psychologist. That was a dilemma.

Class started, and the subject of the lecture was the mind-body connection. The professor, Dr. Blake, was passionate about the subject, but sometimes ventured off onto tangents. Graham found it all fascinating and took meticulous notes.

After class, Graham followed Dr. Blake, a man of about sixty wearing a tweed jacket, back to his office for his office hours. He had been meaning to stop by for quite some time, but he had been preoccupied with falling in love with Gina. The call from Kaya the night before had reminded him to make a better effort. He waited outside the office until his teacher got settled, and then he knocked on the door and walked in. "Professor Blake?"

Dr. Blake looked up from his desk. "Oh, hello," he said. "Are you here for office hours? I so rarely get anyone here until it's time for exams. Have we met? You look familiar."

Graham smiled. "I'm in your Abnormal Psych class. You know, the one you just came from. I'm Graham Reed." He reached out his hand.

Dr. Blake looked at his hand with an amused smile and then accepted it. "Nice to meet you, Mr. Reed. Have a seat. How can I help you today?"

"Um," Graham said, shifting uncomfortably in his chair. "I wanted to talk to you about something of a personal nature."

Dr. Blake's face went blank. "Are you having some mental health issues, Mr. Reed? Because if you are, I need to tell you that I'm not a psychiatrist. You'll need to go see someone at the health center. Have you been there? It's on the west campus. They're very nice over there."

Graham shook his head. "No," he said. "I don't have any symptoms of mental illness, but thank you for your concern. I do have a family member who has some very puzzling symptoms, though, and she has been seen by a psychiatrist, and put on medication, but she's off them now. I'm trying to learn as much as I can about her condition, and that's what got me interested in learning about abnormal psych."

Dr. Blake nodded. "I'm willing to bet that ninety-nine percent of people in the social service business got involved due to some personal connection. Me, it was my grandfather. Bipolar disorder. Made my mother's life miserable as a child. I swore I would make it up to the world by learning how to beat it. It turns out you can't beat it. You just have to find the best way to treat it. Not the best news. What's the deal with your relative?"

"Voices," Graham said.

"Schizophrenia?" the professor asked.

Graham shook his head. "No," he said. "Just voices. And really weird voices. Nothing like what I've read about." He outlined the symptoms to his teacher.

"I've never in my life heard of anything like that," Dr. Blake said. "Are you sure that's what's going on? She's not making things up, or lying to you? Could she be minimizing other symptoms she has?"

Graham shook his head again. "No, she's not lying. She's been really consistent for the last two years. I've seen her when it happens. She really believes that people are saying these things. And usually they're just conversational. Except for the one time that the girl was threatening her. And what's weird is that one of the things that she said she heard actually happened the next year. She heard the girl say she was going to put a laxative in *her* milk, and then later, the girl did something similar to someone else."

"She must have heard her say it to someone else another time, and just forgot."

Graham shook his head. "No, she didn't. The girl didn't tell anyone. Kaya never heard anything else talk about it except the one specific time, but no one else heard it. Kaya's friends with everyone. I mean *everyone*. Someone would have told her if they had heard her being threatened."

"She's friends with everyone?" the professor asked. "Huh. She really doesn't sound like your typical psychotic. Yeah, I'm stymied. I would love to get my hands on her medical records. What was her diagnosis?"

"Auditory hallucinations."

"That's not a diagnosis," Dr. Blake said.

"I know," Graham said. "I told her the same thing. I think the psychiatrist didn't want to give her a diagnosis that she really didn't fit into."

"Can I meet your sister?"

Graham shook his head. "She's in Wisteria."

"Oh, that is a problem. Damn. She would make a wonderful research paper. Tenure, you know."

Graham nodded. "She might come here in two years," he said. "Maybe you can meet with her then. If she's up for it. She'll probably be really busy. She's a cheerleader."

"Of course she is. Huh." Dr. Blake shook his head. "Wow. Well—"

There was a knock on the door. Both men looked up.

"Professor?" a woman asked shyly. "I have a question about the term paper?"

"I'll be with you in just a moment," Dr. Blake said, waving her back into the hallway. He turned back to Graham. "Imagine that. No one has come to my office hours all month. Now two in one day. Young man, we need to talk more about this. Maybe we're on to something. There's not usually anything new in the world of mental health. It's pretty much the same things over and over, with slight variations from person to person. Nothing like what you've seen, or if there is, I haven't seen anything published about it. I want to get to the bottom of what's going on with this young lady. I want to keep in touch. How can I find you?"

"Uh, in your Abnormal Psych class on Tuesday and Thursday afternoons. I sit near the front. I never miss a class."

"Right," Dr. Blake said, getting to his feet. "Today's Thursday. So I'll see you on Tuesday. I'll be talking about biological aspects of mental illness. If anything new comes up with your sister by then, let me know. In the meantime, take notes. If this all works out, I might let you coauthor the paper with me."

"Or maybe we could find a way to help my sister," Graham said.

"Oh yes," the professor said, nodding. "That, too." He reached out to shake Graham's hand again. "It was a pleasure to meet you, Mr. Graham."

"It's Mr. Reed," Graham corrected. "First name Graham."

"Yes, it is," Dr. Blake said. "Don't you forget it."

CHAPTER 9

Kaya: Senior Year

"SO YEAH, I APPLIED TO State," Kaya told Gina, "but I also applied to a ton of East Coast schools. I love the Big East, and it would be amazing to cheer for one of those schools. Georgetown, Syracuse, Villanova, Providence . . . all of those are great schools, but I don't know if I'd be able to get a scholarship. Some of the cheerleaders from bigger cities had professional choreographers all four years, and even nicer uniforms. The playing field isn't really even."

"But you're so good," Gina said. "I saw your videos. You're the best senior on the team. And Graham says everyone really respects you on the team. I would love it if you went to State. We'd be able to see you much more often."

"Who wants hot chocolate?" Mrs. Reed asked, coming into the living room, skirting the Christmas tree, and putting the tray down on the table. "That was a rhetorical question. You all told me who wanted it just fifteen minutes ago." She sat on the couch next to Kaya and put her arm around her back. "What are you all talking about?"

"College," Kaya said, leaning forward to pick up a steaming mug. "And where I'm going next year. I know it all depends on scholarships. No matter where I go, I'll make the most of it. I mean, I don't think I want to be a professional cheerleader after college. I'll probably hang up my pompoms when I graduate."

Graham laughed. "I have the best image in my mind of you literally hanging up pompoms. But even if you don't cheer professionally, you could teach dance, or coach a team or something. You don't have to give it up entirely."

Kaya shrugged. "True. Or maybe someday I'll have a daughter, and she'll be interested in dancing or cheering. And I could give her a few pointers."

Mrs. Reed sighed. "I can't believe my last baby's leaving the nest next year," she said. "I'll be home by myself for the first time. I don't know how I feel about it. I guess I'll either love it or hate it. Maybe I should find a boyfriend to keep me company."

Graham's head whipped around and he stared at his mother. "Really?"

Mrs. Reed gave him a look. "Graham, I don't think I'm meant to be alone forever. I deserve to have someone in my life. I really don't think Peter's ever coming home. It's been over three years. If I'd wanted to, I could have him declared dead by now."

She looked at Kaya, whose eyes had gone wide. Mrs. Reed's brows came together.

"I'm sorry, Kaya. That wasn't very sensitive of me. I didn't mean anything by it. I don't think he's dead. I'm just saying that at some point, I might want to dissolve our marriage so I can be free to have love in my life again. I've never stopped loving your father, but there does come a time—"

Kaya waved her hand. "You don't have to explain," she said. "It was just the word *dead*. It just hit me. I wonder sometimes where he is. He's kind of like Schrodinger's cat; in my mind he's both alive and dead, and we won't know until we open the box. But we can't open the box because we don't know where it is. It's so frustrating."

Graham listened to the conversation with interest.

"I don't know," he said. "I think if he were dead, someone would have notified us by now. I like to think of him as being in a big canvas tent in the desert, or a yurt in the woods, or something, living off the grid. No cell phone, and maybe a helicopter comes over every week and does a food drop. Total isolation."

"Sometimes I think I would like total isolation," Kaya said quietly.

Everyone looked at her. "Why is that, Kaya?" her mother asked.

"Because it's quiet," she said. "Totally quiet. I'd never have to worry about hearing anything weird or bizarre. When I'm alone, it's quiet."

"Is it always noisy when you hear things?" Gina asked.

"Not always noisy," Kaya said. "But usually busy, or crowded. There are other conversations going on, and people up close. Sometimes, I hear a bunch of things at the same time and have to figure out what's real and what's the voices. Have you ever been to a party and there are tons of people all talking at the same time, and it's hard to focus on just one conversation? Sometimes you can pare it down and listen to the person you're facing, but other times, it just sounds like noise. Yeah, that's kind of what it's like."

Gina shivered. "That sounds a bit scary."

Kaya shook her head. "It's never scary. It's really just like things everyone else hears, but out of context. I bet you've experienced it. And when I hear the voices clearly, they say things like, 'I wonder if Patrick noticed my zit in chemistry class,' or 'I'm so hungry, I could chew my own right arm off right now.' From what Graham tells me, a lot of people with voices hear things that are scary, like threats, or insults. And sometimes they tell people to do bad things. I don't have any of that."

"It's so weird," Gina said. "When Graham first told me about your voices, I kind of dreaded meeting you. But then I met you, and you're just like everyone else. I would never have known if Graham hadn't told me."

Kaya smiled. "I guess I get away with it. I did hear someone once say that he was going to break up with his girlfriend after school. It made me so sad. I had to keep reminding myself that it was just a voice. But the strange thing was, they *did* break up. I don't know if it happened that very day, but it was soon after. Sometimes I wonder . . ." She trailed off.

"Don't go there, Kaya," Mrs. Reed said quickly. "Don't go down that rabbit hole of thinking that what you're hearing is real. That's only gonna cause you trouble. Remember what Dr. Colton said: the voices come from a part of your brain that creates language, and the voices can sound very real, but it's coming from your own brain. You have to treat them like a story that your brain is telling you. But it's not a true story."

Kaya pursed her lips and closed her eyes. "I know, Mom," she said in an annoyed voice. "I was there, too, and I heard his clever explanation. Yes. It's my tricky little brain. I get that. But even he can't explain why I am the way I am. No one can. I'm a medical mystery."

"I've heard that they can do these MRIs that can scan people while they're doing things," Gina said. "They're called functional MRIs. They show where the brain lights up when a person is subjected to certain stimuli. So they're able to tell what part of the brain is working at the time. It would be cool if you could do one of those, Kaya."

Kaya's face lit up. "That sounds so cool. How do you get to do things like that?"

"Dr. Blake talked about that in my Abnormal Psych class," Graham said. "He said they aren't used in medical practice. They're mostly for research. A lot of universities have them. It would be cool to get involved with that type of research. The brain is so interesting."

"Maybe when I'm in college, I can sign up for some of that research," Kaya said.

Graham nodded. "I know that Dr. Blake would love to meet you and learn more about your brain."

Kaya stiffened visibly. "You told him about me?"

Graham gritted his teeth. He knew he had made a mistake by saying that. But now it was too late. "Yeah," he said. "He knows so much stuff. I thought he might have some ideas. So last winter, I went to his office and gave him your history. He said he'd never heard of anyone like you, at least in the reading that he's done."

Kaya sneered at Graham. "Please don't do things like that, Graham," she said firmly. "It's my life, and my story. You can't just go talking about me without getting my permission! What if I end up going to State, and I meet this guy? Now I'm not just another student. I'm an interesting research subject." She sighed. "I'm not mad at you, Graham. I know that you only meant to help. Just next time, okay?"

Graham nodded ruefully. "I'm sorry, Ky. But the good news is, he does want to learn more. So if you do go to State, maybe you can meet with him, and he can help us find some answers. Maybe he can even do one of those functional MRIs on you."

"Does State even have one of those?"

Graham shrugged. "I have no idea. I haven't seen Dr. Blake since I took his class two semesters ago. I guess I could seek him out and find out. If you want, you can come up and stay with us for a long weekend and I can arrange for you to meet him."

Kaya tilted her head. "Maybe."

Mrs. Reed shook her head. "I'm not sure how I feel about this," she said. "This guy isn't a medical doctor, Kaya, and you're not a lab animal. I would like to know more about him, that he's legit. And I would want to know if he's gonna write a paper about you. I need to make sure your confidentiality is respected. Someday, you're gonna want to get a job, and you don't want to be known as the enigma with the auditory hallucinations."

Kaya laughed. "I think it would be funny to be known as The Enigma! That could be my superhero name!"

Now Graham laughed. "I love that idea. If you don't become famous due to your freaky brain issue, you can become a famous comic book writer. I wonder what other super powers The Enigma would have. Magic lasso?" He nudged Gina in the ribs and watched her turn a bright shade of red.

Kaya thought about it. "She would be able to fly like Superman, breathe underwater like Aqua Man, and have super strength like The Hulk. And she would be able to hear secret messages as they passed through the air. She would be a super spy!"

"Can I design her costume?" Gina piped in. "I already have some ideas. The Enigma would have crazy colors and patterns. No cape. Really cool knee-high boots."

"Would you all cut it out please?" Mrs. Reed insisted. "This isn't a joke. Kaya, I know you like to make light of it, but this is your life! Please don't reduce it to something so trivial. You know what? I'm done with my cocoa.

Can you all clean up after yourselves when you're done? I'm going up to get ready for bed."

She stood, and with no further ado, she headed up the stairs.

Everyone watched the stairs long after she was gone. Then Gina turned to Graham. "What was that all about?"

"She doesn't think it's funny," Kaya said. "I've tried to keep it light over the years, you know, making jokes about it to try to convince her that I'm okay. When I finally came clean to her that I had stopped my medication last year, she was so mad. She thought I was playing fast and loose with my life, and that I was being irresponsible. She didn't think I was old or mature enough to make my own decisions. But I told her that she couldn't stop me. I wasn't going to take the medication. I think I took away her power." She slumped in her seat. "I didn't mean to. It just happened."

Graham stared at his sister. "Wow," he said. "I had no idea all of this was going on." He paused.

"I wonder if it would have been any different if—"

"I know," Kaya said. "I wonder the same thing. Dad."

Gina pulled Graham to his feet, and they both went over to sit with Kaya on the couch, one on either side.

"I'm sorry, Kaya," she said. "I joined in with you guys with the joking. It's really not my place to do that."

Graham shook his head. "That's not true, Gina. Aside from medical professionals, the only people who know our deep dark family secret are Mom, Kaya, me, you, and Dr. Blake. You're just as much a part of this as the rest of us."

"It's true," Kaya said, reaching out and grasping Gina's arm. "You're part of the insanity now. There's no escape from the Reed family." She chuckled. "Except for Dad, of course."

"There you go again," Graham teased. "Not taking any of this stuff seriously."

"Graham," Kaya said, putting her arm around her brother. "If I took any of this stuff seriously, I seriously would go crazy."

Later that night, Graham and Gina crawled into their bed in Graham's childhood bedroom.

"Do you think that Dr. Blake would really be interested in meeting Kaya?" Gina asked.

"I do," Graham said. "Don't you remember how he chased me down after my final exam last year and told me to keep in touch? He handed me his business card. I think he's really intrigued by Kaya, or at least what she might represent. It would be like an archaeologist finding the lost continent of Atlantis, to find something new in the mental health field. And he's really close to retiring. It would be his swan song."

"A mental health swan song," Gina said with a smile. "It would be pretty cool to go out with a splash when you retire. It's better than getting kicked to the curb for being obsolete."

Graham laughed. "I haven't even started a career yet," he said. "It's impossible to even imagine what retirement would be like. I wish we could just skip all the work stuff and retire at twenty-one."

"Yeah," Gina agreed. "It would make more sense to have retirement when you're young enough to enjoy it. You know what they say: youth is wasted on the young. Maybe retirement is wasted on the old."

Graham snuggled closer to his girlfriend and put his arm behind her neck. "I would love to retire with you. Someday, we will retire together. But yeah, if we retired now, we could have so much fun. We could travel and see the world, or stay home and build a great house with a great yard and garden. And we could have kids and not have to worry about daycare."

"Daycare," Gina repeated. "Can you imagine? We'll have to get really good jobs after college to start saving up for daycare so we can put our kids into daycare so we can work, to be able to afford daycare."

"We should think about starting a savings account now," Graham said. He kissed Gina's cheek. "When do you think we should tell them that we're engaged? Should we wait until Christmas morning, or should we be a little less dramatic?"

"Dramatic?" Gina asked. "You mean like pulling up in front of Wisteria High School and proposing to me right in front of the main doors, while the students were still in school and all gawking at us?"

Graham grinned. "It was the right thing to do. I owe that school a lot, you know."

Gina snuggled into his arms. "I think we should tell them tomorrow. That way we don't take anything away from everyone else's Christmas. Plus, they would be expecting it on Christmas. Let's catch them off guard."

The next morning, Graham got up before Gina. He knew his mother always kept orange juice in the fridge, and the thought of drinking some became obsessive. He pulled on a T-shirt and his pajama pants and made his way downstairs.

Kaya was already in the kitchen. "Hey, Graham," she said as she poured herself a glass of juice. "Want some?"

"That's what I came here for," he said, taking a glass from her. "Why are you up so early?"

"Last-minute Christmas shopping with Rayna," she said, putting an English muffin in the toaster. "She needs to get something pretty special for Jeff. She applied for colleges in Georgia, and he's not happy about it."

"They're still together?" Graham asked. He took a big gulp of juice, savoring the flavor as it ran over his tongue and down his throat.

"Yup," Kaya said, taking the raspberry jam out of the fridge. "I knew they were into each other back then, and they still are. But I think Jeff's worried about having a long-distance relationship."

"Did he tell you that?" Graham asked, looking at her sideways.

Kaya looked down. "No."

"So how do you know?" Graham asked. "Or do I want to ask?"

"The same way I know that you and Gina are engaged."

Graham almost dropped his glass. "What? How did you know that?"

Kaya's eyes went wide. "So it's true?"

"Kaya," Graham said, taking a step toward her. "Did you hear me and Gina talking in my room last night?"

Kaya shook her head. "I think I fell asleep before you even came upstairs."

"So . . ."

"Yeah," Kaya said. "You told me yourself."

"Wh-what did I say?" Graham asked, his voice shaky.

"You said, 'They're gonna be really excited when I tell them.' That's all you said."

"When did I say that?"

"On the couch last night. After Mom took off upstairs, and you and Gina came and sat with me on the couch. Gina was making happy giddy noises. I can't even describe them. I put two and two together, and came up with a proposal. When did you do it?"

Graham was speechless. This made no sense. The voices were caused by misfiring connections inside of Kaya's brain. There was no way that she knew his thoughts. There had to be another answer. Maybe it was obvious on their faces that something was going on, and Kaya figured it out that way, therefore influencing the content of her voices. That had to be it. She figured it out subconsciously. Maybe she and their mother were expecting them to get engaged over Christmas. Graham accepted that explanation. That had to be it.

"It was yesterday afternoon," he said. "We went by the high school, and I proposed to her there."

Kaya smiled. "Scene of the crime." She hugged Graham. "I'm so happy for you, brother. The two of you are a great couple, and I'm so glad Gina's gonna be part of our family. When were you planning on telling us?"

"This morning during breakfast," Graham said. "And that's still the plan. Don't you dare tell Gina you know, okay? Let's keep this our secret. Can you act surprised when we tell you?"

Kaya frowned. "Graham, I'm sorry I spoiled your surprise. But yeah, I'll act surprised. As a matter of fact, I can't even remember what we were talking about. Surprised about what? I don't know anything!" She smiled happily and touched her finger to her nose.

Graham touched his finger to his nose, too, and smiled back. But he was feeling unsettled. Even though he had figured out a way to explain how Kaya had found out about the engagement, the whole situation was nagging at his brain.

"Kaya . . . I'm thinking of a number between one and ten. What is it?"

Kaya closed her eyes. Then she opened them and shook her head. "I don't know," she said. "Five?"

Graham shook his head. "No," he said. "It was seven."

There was something going on here, and Graham wanted to know what it was. He decided that as soon as he got back to school, he was going to find Dr. Blake's card and give him a call. It was time to find some answers.

Chapter 10

THE LOOK ON KAYA'S FACE was different from the other times she had gotten out of the car at the State University campus. She looked around with new eyes.

"It looks different when it's gonna be my school, too," she told Graham. "It looks bigger, more threatening. Like, that building over there? What if I have a class in there, but I can't find it, and I go into the one over there instead? Man, I hope I don't ever have one class after another. How could you cross the whole campus in what, five minutes?"

Graham smiled at her warmly. "It's not that bad," he assured her. "Yeah, sometimes I have a long way to go between classes, but you can control your schedule. I've never had classes any closer than thirty minutes apart. The bell doesn't ring like it does in high school. Different classes start at different times, and they have different lengths. You'll be fine. I'll take you to my psych class tomorrow so you can see what it's like."

"But you're a junior," Kaya protested. "It will be like jumping from twelfth to fifteenth grade in one day."

Graham laughed. "I bet you'll be able to follow a psych class. Maybe we'll talk about auditory hallucinations tomorrow. You have first-hand experience."

"Yeah, but I'm not gonna say a word." She hefted her backpack to her shoulder. "Let's go in. I can't wait to see where you and Gina live."

They walked across the parking lot, and Graham led Kaya through a walkway and then a courtyard. They walked up two outside flights of stairs, and then Graham unlocked the door. They stepped inside. "You'll sleep on the couch," Graham said. "It pulls out into a bed. It's really comfortable. One time when Gina had a bad cold, I had to sleep in it because I had a final the next day. I slept like a baby. Plus, I didn't have to hear her hacking up a lung all night."

"I notice you only say things like that when she's not around," Kaya said as she dropped her bag on the couch. "This place is small, but it's okay." She walked to the refrigerator and opened the door. "I see you have more than just mustard. It's obvious that a woman lives here. Is that a bag of carrots?"

"We eat pretty well around here," Graham said. He took an apple out of a bowl on the counter and handed it to her. "Wash it first."

Kaya rinsed off the apple, rubbed it on her shirt to dry it, and took a bite. "So where did you say Gina is?" she asked, still chewing her mouthful of apple.

"She's doing an internship," Graham said, giving her a look of disgust. "Do you always talk with your mouth full? Maybe that's why you don't have a boyfriend."

Kaya gave him a pouty look. "Low blow, bro," she said. "But it just so happens, I did meet someone recently." She gave him a little smile.

"Met someone?" he asked. "Where did you meet him?"

Kaya shrugged. "At school. Where else? I don't know how I missed him, but all of a sudden, there he was in the lunch line. There was only one pudding left, and we both reached for it at the same time. Our hands touched. It was like the movies. Chemistry. Tingles and everything."

"Wow," Graham said. "Huh. What's his name?"

"Grayson. Isn't that a great name?"

"If you're a vampire," Graham teased. "Is he a senior too?"

"Yes. But he wasn't hiding the whole time. He moved to Wisteria at the beginning of junior year. He's not a huge sports fan, so he never saw me cheering. He just likes pudding. But he let me take the last one. And the funny thing? You know how I usually hear voices around guys and it puts me off of them? This time, the voice was really positive."

"What did it say?" Graham asked.

"He said, 'Wow.'"

"Wow?"

"Yeah." Kaya sighed. "That's all I needed to hear. What else does a girl want to hear? *Wow*. Yeah, I agreed. Wow."

"What does Mom think about Mr. Wowser?" Graham asked.

"She likes him," Kaya said. "She had me ask him over for dinner a few weeks ago. It went really well."

Graham shook his head. "Why didn't you tell me about him before?"

Kaya shrugged. "I figured I'd be here soon and I could tell you face to face. Like now."

Graham nodded. "Okay." He took a seat on the couch. "So what about your, well, your issue? Have you told him about it?"

Kaya looked uncomfortable. "Sort of," she said. "I told him that sometimes I can tell what other people are thinking."

"Kaya! If you're gonna talk about it, you should at least tell him the truth!"

"I will," she said, defensively. "But it's not as easy as it sounds."

Graham rolled his eyes. "Kaya, I'm not saying it's easy at all," he said. "I don't think it would be easy at all. But you know what's harder? Having to take back a lie. And explain why you lied. The way I see it is you could tell the truth or he can find out that you lied on his own. Both ways, he knows the truth."

Kaya bit her bottom lip. "I know you're right. But sometimes, it does feel more like I have a special power than an illness. Sometimes, I have to remind myself that I'm not hearing people's thoughts. It's their voices, and what they say is mostly unexpected, like things they don't want other people to hear. You know. Like hidden thoughts. Secrets."

Graham blinked and nodded. "I know," he said softly. "It's appealing to think about it that way." He smiled at her. "But The Enigma is sworn to tell the truth at all times. She wears Wonder Woman's Lasso of Truth around her waist as a belt."

Kaya laughed. "Should we make dinner for Gina before she gets home?"

Graham nodded. "What's your specialty?"

Kaya gave him an exaggerated smile. "You got ingredients for pancakes?"

"I have no idea what to say to him," Kaya said as she followed Graham down the hallway toward Dr. Blake's office. "I mean, he's like a hundred years old. Does he even speak modern English?"

Graham gave her a look of disbelief. "He's like sixty-three, maybe," he said. "He's younger than Grandpa. You talk to Grandpa all the time."

"I know," Kaya said, wringing her hands. "But Grandpa doesn't have a PhD. Grandpa likes to talk about pickling onions. This guy knows about brains and stuff. And what's inside them."

"He's just a guy," Graham told her. "And he's kind of eccentric. He might know about neurotransmitters and synapses, but he can't find the cap to his coffee thermos. He wears a tweed blazer. I don't think they even make tweed anymore." He stopped in front of a closed door. "Here we are. Are you ready?"

A flash of panic came across Kaya's face. She ran her fingers through her bangs. "Do I look okay?"

Graham smiled at her. "You look beautiful. Like always. But I think Dr. Blake is married."

Kaya smirked and smacked him on the arm. "I don't know if you'll get a better grade in your class because you're bringing me to meet your professor," she said suddenly.

Graham stared at her. "Why would you say that?"

Kaya shrugged. "I know you weren't really thinking that, but that's what your voice just told me. But I could understand you actually thinking that. I mean, not like you're using me for a grade, but if you get a better grade, that's a nice perk."

Graham furrowed his brow. He thought about it. Yeah, it probably was something he would think. But had he just been thinking it? He couldn't remember if he had. He shrugged and then he knocked on the door.

"Come in!"

Graham opened the door. "Dr. Blake? Hi. I brought my sister to meet you." He ushered Kaya into the office. "Kaya, this is Dr. Blake. Dr. Blake, this is my sister, Kaya."

As Dr. Blake stood, a smile spread across his face. He stuck out his hand. "It's wonderful to meet you, Kaya. Reed here says you'll be attending State next year."

"It's Graham. Last name Reed."

"Yes," Dr. Blake said. "I have to check every now and then to make sure you remember."

Kaya smiled and reached out shyly for Dr. Blake's hand. "Nice to meet you," she said softly. She stared at Dr. Blake.

Graham observed his sister. The look was somewhat familiar. She was hearing a voice. She was hearing Dr. Blake's voice. Her smile grew, and then she let go of his hand.

"Have a seat," Dr. Blake said, motioning for them to sit in the two seats in front of his desk. "Do either of you want coffee? It's from this morning. I can rewarm it if you want."

"No thanks," Kaya said confidently.

Dr. Blake nodded. "So I saw you in class with Graham this morning," he said. "Did you enjoy the lecture?"

Kaya nodded. "A lot of it was above my head, but it was interesting."

"Yes, the brain is fascinating. I hear that you have a fascinating brain yourself, young lady."

Kaya squirmed slightly. "That's what they tell me."

"I'd like to hear more about it," Dr. Blake said, lacing his fingers together in front of him. "Graham said that you would like to learn more, too. He said you would be interested in being part of a study, including some testing on the fMRI."

Kaya nodded. "Yes. Since I first heard about it, I've done some reading, and I'm really curious. My doctor did a regular MRI on me a few years ago, and everything looked pretty normal, but he said there was a slight enlargement of the structure of my receptive language area of the temporal lobe. He said it appeared to be congenital. He did a repeat last year, and there were no changes. He didn't think it would be responsible for causing auditory hallucinations, but he's not a neurologist. I was always curious as to why he didn't refer me to a neurologist. He just sent me right to a psychiatrist. It seems that once someone makes up their mind that you're crazy, there's no other way to go but the psych route. I could go into an ER today with a knife coming out of my back, and they'd probably just focus on asking me if I'm hearing voices."

"Yes, the stigma." Dr. Blake sighed. "My family had to deal with it with my grandfather. At one point, when he was old and had health problems, we had to decide if we were going to have him move into an assisted living facility, but no one wanted to take him due to his diagnosis of bipolar disorder, and the fact that he was hospitalized several times as a younger man. We ended up having to have him live with us until he died, which was seven years. It was extremely hard on my mother. I vowed to do everything I could to break the stigma when I had a voice that people would listen to. And now I have that voice, and I'm using it."

Kaya looked at Dr. Blake in awe. "You're a superhero," she said. "When I find my band of cohorts, I'm going to invite you to join us. I'm The Enigma. You'll need to choose your own superhero name."

Dr. Blake chuckled. "I'll give it some thought. No one has ever called me a superhero. Nerd, yes. Superhero, no. But I'll be retiring in the next two years. I've always wanted to be on the cutting edge of some new, groundbreaking discovery. Now, Kaya, I don't know if that's where we're headed. I don't want to get your hopes up that we're going to discover something that no one has discovered before and find a way to fix it. But every little bit of information we get goes a long way in helping us form the bigger picture. Every bit of data counts. Your symptoms are unusual. Learning more about your condition might not lead to helping you, you understand, but it might help someone ten, twenty years from now. And not just someone. Lots of someones. How do you feel about that?"

Kaya bit her lip. "I'd like to help myself, but I've already learned that medication isn't the way I want to go. I know there are probably a lot of people out there that don't want to take meds, but they don't have any other option. Most of them don't have the same advantages that I have.

Their symptoms are worse, more distressing. So if I can help them, yeah, I'm on board."

Dr. Blake smiled. "Excellent," he said. "We can spend some time together today gathering some basic information about your medical history and your experiences with the auditory hallucinations. I have some brief questionnaires for you to fill out about your symptoms, or lack thereof. Why don't you do those first and get them over with, and then we'll have a discussion about everything else."

He handed Kaya a clipboard and a pen and gave her an encouraging grin.

"While you fill this out, I'll be under my desk, looking for my wallet. It seems to have gone missing again. I hate when my things grow legs and walk away."

"So what did Dr. Blake's voice say?" Graham asked after they left the office an hour later.

"What?" Kaya asked.

"You know," Graham said. "When I introduced you. You were all nervous, and then you shook his hand, and when you were done, you stared at him and smiled. What did his voice say?"

Kaya laughed. "Oh my God. You can tell when I'm hearing the voices? That's so wild! But yeah, I was feeling really shaky, but then when we were shaking hands, his voice told me that he was really nervous about meeting me. Can you believe it? Nervous about meeting me? I'm a seventeen year old high school kid!"

Graham laughed. "Yeah, but could you imagine what he was like back in high school? Cheerleaders probably never gave him the time of day! He was probably feeling kind of out of his league." Graham shook his head. "Kaya, you even got me forgetting that it's not his real thoughts. It was his voice, but not his thoughts. But it seems like it put you at ease, so I guess it doesn't matter. I bet there's no one else in the world who gets comfort from their hallucinations like you do."

"Maybe," Kaya said. They left the building, and she looked across the quad. "Let's go look at some of the other buildings. Where did you have the most classes freshman year?"

Graham pointed to a three-story brick building. "This is the Sawyer Building. It has the biggest lecture halls. Let's go inside. I bet there's an empty one we can go into."

Graham led Kaya into the building, past students sitting on the stairs reading or talking to their friends. In the entryway, there was a mob of students milling around holding backpacks or notebooks. Almost every one of them was holding a cup of takeout coffee.

"I guess coffee's a big part of college life," Kaya said. "I wonder if that coffee cart serves hot chocolate or chai tea."

"They have hot chocolate," Graham confirmed. "We must be the only kids in North America that grew up with parents that didn't drink coffee. You would think that we would have rebelled by drinking all the coffee. Gina likes it though, so I'm trying to learn to like it."

"Maybe I could learn to like it." She was looking closely at the handsome man behind the counter at the coffee cart.

Graham laughed. "What about Grayson?"

Kaya looked at him. "Grayson? He doesn't like coffee either." She gave him a sly smile.

Graham laughed again. "C'mon," he said. "I'll show you the lecture hall." He walked through a door, and Kaya followed him in. "This is where I took my introduction to philosophy class."

Kaya's eyes widened as she took in the massive hall. "Wow!" she exclaimed. "This place is bigger than the gym at Wisteria High! How many students are in these classes?"

"Around two hundred," Graham said.

Kaya shook her head. "Oh my God! So, if you don't show up for class, no one knows?"

"That's right," Graham said. "I've missed a class or two over the years. You just have to make sure you find out what you missed. You'll get a syllabus in each class, and it should tell you about what's being covered every week, if not every single class, and a list of all of your assignments, but it's always good to make friends in your classes, so you can ask them if there was anything you need to know in the lecture. You can make copies of their notes."

Kaya sat down in one of the stadium seats. "Close seating," she said. "It's like a movie theater. Is there enough room to move around?"

Graham took the seat next to her. "I guess," he said. "I mean, yeah, your arm might be up against the person next to you, like on an airplane. But it's only for an hour or so. You'll get through it."

Kaya nodded but she wasn't smiling.

"What are you worried about?"

Kaya shrugged. "It's just close quarters. You know. Close quarters."

Graham suddenly understood. "More voices in close quarters." Kaya nodded. "Yikes."

"Yeah." Kaya looked at her shoes. Then she looked up and around the room. "Maybe I can figure out how to make it not so bad. I can sit at the end of the row, so I can get up and get out if I need to. Maybe I can sit near the back or stand against the wall. Oh, I could sit on the floor in the back. They use microphones, right?"

Graham felt a stab in his heart. He couldn't believe all of the thought that had to go into where Kaya would sit during her classes. All he ever had to do was walk in and find an empty seat. And he only had to focus on one voice, the one giving the lecture. Kaya always talked like she was fine, and that her voices didn't disrupt her life at all. But maybe they really did. Maybe Kaya didn't realize it because it was all she had known for several years now. Graham swallowed. His throat felt tight. He put his arm around her shoulder protectively. She looked up at him, searching his eyes. Then, she relaxed against him and let her head rest on his shoulder.

"It will be okay, Graham," she said softly. "It always is. I promise."

$\mathcal{C}$HAPTER 11

Kaya: Palmetto State, Freshman Year

GRAHAM LOOKED AROUND THE ROOM. "It's really nice," he said. "I didn't get into Paulson Hall freshman year. I ended up living with mostly sophomores. I'm glad you got the freshman dorm."

Kaya put a framed picture of herself and Grayson at the prom on the shelf above her bed. "That looks good there," she said. She smiled. "I think the place looks great, don't you?"

"It does," Graham said. He sat on the bed and bounced up and down a little. "Even the beds are more comfortable here. And how did you get Mom to buy you a nice comforter? I had to bring the one I had in my bedroom at home."

Kaya shrugged. "I'm her special child," she said with a grin. "I just had to ask nicely." She took an old, wrinkled family picture out of her last box and tacked it to her corkboard. "Hello, young Dad," she said to it. "Welcome to my dorm room." She turned away and went back to the box. "I hope my roommate isn't a slob. I want to try to keep my room neat and orderly, just like my life." She laughed. "Okay, I'll keep it neat and orderly, despite my life."

"Are you gonna make new friends while you're here," Graham asked, "or are you just gonna hang out with Grayson all the time?"

"Both," Kaya answered quickly. "I'm gonna make new friends *with* Grayson. We're gonna do everything we can. We're gonna join clubs, and go to games. I mean, when I'm not at cheerleading practice or actually working a game. We've decided that we'll be popular here. I know I was well liked at Wisteria High, but I mostly hung out with Cat, Bailey, and Rayna. And most of the time, it was one of them at a time. I want to try to have a group of friends here that I can hang out with."

"That sounds like a good idea," Graham said. "I made a few friends at first, but then when Gina and I got together, it was easier to just be with her all the time. She felt the same way. The next year, we had to work really hard to branch out. I'm glad we did, though. Gina would probably have burned out on me a long time ago if we hadn't."

"I don't know about that," Kaya said. She sat down beside him. "Do you think Mom will really be all right with both of us gone?"

"She will," Graham assured her. "Maybe she'll actually like it. Now that she was able to get a legal divorce from Dad, she's free to start dating, and she doesn't have to worry about being around for us all the time."

Kaya shook her head. "Dating. I can't imagine Mom on a date. Who would she even date? Does she even know any men? Maybe she can date Mr. Grace, the gym teacher at Wisteria. He's nice, and I'm pretty sure he's single."

"*I'm* pretty sure that Mr. Grace and Mr. Beech are more than just chums that watch sports together on weekends," Graham said.

"Oh. Huh. I had no idea. Rayna had a crush on Mr. Beech freshman year. Man, Wisteria is so small. Mom will probably have to go out to Florence or Garrison to meet anyone."

"She met Dad," Graham said. "He was just passing through town when they met. Maybe someone else will pass through town and she'll meet him. Otherwise, she'll have to take trips to the city every now and then. Or she can join a dating service. Lots of people are meeting people online these days."

"It seems kind of weird to me," Kaya said. "I like to meet people face to face. You know, so I can see the expressions on their faces when they tell me things, so I can tell if they're telling the truth."

"How can you tell?" Graham asked.

Kaya shrugged. "Sometimes, it's in their eyes. Sometimes, it's the way they breathe. Like, people breathe slower when they're telling the truth. And of course, their tone of voice." She looked out the window. "Look, there are still a lot of people arriving. I thought they told people to get here before three."

"I think that's just a guideline," Graham said. "But let's get back to their tone of voice. What about it?"

"I . . . I guess it's the pitch. You know, if it's higher or lower. And if they trip over their words. And how fast they talk. Some people talk fast, but if someone who talks slow suddenly talks fast, that's a warning sign."

"So," Graham said, standing and starting to pace the length of the room, "are you talking about the talking they do when their lips move?"

Kaya's face turned red. "What difference does it make?" She stood too. "You know, sometimes, I don't understand you, Graham. You're so worried about me all the time, about my voices. Why can't you just trust me? I mean, I've done fine for years! So what if sometimes I listen to the voices, and trust them? I really think it's possible that my mind creates the voices from my own instincts. I look at someone, or I see something happening, and then I hear the person say what I feel they're thinking. Yeah, they're not actually saying it, but maybe my brain is interpreting what they might say. And it works for me."

She started to pace beside Graham.

"For instance, I figured out that Jeff liked Rayna by what I heard his voice say to me. And I was right. And I 'heard' Grayson say wow, and I was right. I pick up cues. You do it too, all the time, but you do it inside your head, and your brain interprets it quietly. I just do it outside my head, and with someone else's voice. Maybe you can start thinking about it like that. That way, none of it matters anymore! I *do* want to work with Dr. Blake once things settle down a bit here, but basically because I want to understand why I'm different. I already know how I'm different, but not why. But think about it. What have I lost by having the voices? I got good grades,

I was the cheerleading captain last year, I have friends, people like me, I have a boyfriend, and I have a really supportive family. I have a good life, Graham. You don't have to give me the third degree every time you think I'm paying attention to my voices."

She walked back over to her bed and sat down. Then she glared at Graham.

Kaya had left Graham speechless. He sat with her words for a few moments. Then he spent a few more moments formulating his response. "You're right."

Kaya waited. And waited. She looked at her watch, and then back at Graham.

"That's it?" she asked. "That's all you're gonna say? I thought for sure you'd have some sort of rebuttal statement."

Graham shrugged. "No, I've got nothing. You're absolutely right. I don't have anything to add, or take away. I'm gonna stop. I have no right to question you anymore. You're doing great, and like you said, you have a good life."

Kaya smiled and then nodded. "I do," she said. "I like my life." She looked up at her family picture, her smile slipping a little. "I mean, it would be better if, you know, some things had never happened, but . . ."

Graham sat down next to her again. "I know." He took her hand. "It's been a long time since he left, but I still want answers. I don't think about it all the time. It's like I had my foot cut off a long time ago, and I'm wearing a prosthetic shoe, and sometimes I forget my foot is gone. Then one day, my shoe gets untied, and I take it off. And there it is. My missing foot."

Kaya laughed. "I know that you didn't mean that to be funny, Graham, but I love it. My missing foot. I want to record an album and name it that. I bet Grayson would be into it, too. He could play the keyboard." She paused, looked at Graham, and then squeezed his hand. "You *will* always be able to protect me, Graham. Don't worry about it. I'll let you."

Graham looked back into her eyes. "Did I just tell you I was worried?" he asked carefully.

Kaya nodded slowly. "You did," she said. "Do you get it? Look at you. You're worried. You were pacing. It's my first day at college. We were having a serious conversation about you letting go of your worry. Doesn't it make sense that my brain would pick up on your cues, and project what I feel from you into the voice I hear?"

Graham had to agree. It made total sense. "Yes," he said confidently. "I get it. I finally get it."

Kaya smiled. Then the doorknob turned on the door to the room, and a young woman walked in shyly, followed by two adults.

"Hi," Kaya said.

The other girl smiled. "I'm Cameron."

Kaya nodded. "I'm Kaya. And this is my brother, Graham. He goes here too. He's a senior."

Graham stood. "Nice to meet you, Cameron," He turned to Kaya. "I'll take off now so you can get acquainted with your roommate." He gave her a hug. "Call me tonight, okay? Gina and I will be home."

Kaya looked up nervously at her brother. "You really don't have to go," she said timidly.

Graham smiled and nodded. "Yes, I do," he said. "It's time for you to be off on your own at college. But I'll never be too far away." He kissed her cheek, and then headed for the door. "I'm sure I'll see you again, Cameron," he said, and then he walked out into the hallway.

It was October, and Graham was starting to think about what he might do after college. He had chosen a path, but he didn't know yet where it would lead him. He enjoyed learning about psychology, but he wasn't sure if he wanted to continue studying it or even work in the field. But he didn't know what other options he had. Gina had been studying elementary education, and she knew exactly what she wanted to do: She wanted to be a kindergarten teacher.

"I love their little faces," Gina said, talking about the children she was working with in her current placement. "They're so small and round. And there's no worry on them. I mean, yeah, someday there will be, but not now. Now they're just like one of those blank books that are so popular, ready to be filled up, and I want to make sure that what fills them up is the truth, positive and focused. I get to help shape minds. And from what I've picked up from psychology, it's not just a metaphor. Their minds are really being developed, one synapsis at a time. I love the look in their eyes when they make a connection."

"It sounds like what you're doing is a lot like what I could be doing," Graham said, handing her four plates to put on the table. "But I don't want to work with kids. They kind of scare me."

He noted the look of horror on Gina's face.

"No," he said quickly. "I don't mean *our* kids will scare me. Other people's kids. The ones that aren't bonded to me. Our kids will be perfectly well-behaved, mentally well geniuses who adore us and listen to everything we tell them."

Gina laughed. "So where are we going to buy these perfect kids?" she asked. "But if you don't want to work with kids, you shouldn't. You would do well with adults. You're intelligent, and you take other people seriously. You're a good listener. You'd make a good therapist if you wanted to be one. I know you don't know if you want to be one, but I think you'd be great. You'd be great at anything you wanted to be."

Graham stirred the simmering pot on the stove. "I want to be a hockey player," he said. Then he laughed. "I could sweep the street after parades. I could be president of the United States, but I'd have to find something else I can do until I'm thirty-five. Uh, do you need to go to culinary school to become a pastry chef?"

Gina smiled as she finished setting the table. "I think you might. But if that's what you want to do, I'll support you. But I think you'd be happier doing something where you can use all the knowledge you've accumulated the last three and a half years. Maybe you could be a research assistant, and then go back to school later if you like doing research so you can do your own projects."

Graham nodded. "Where did you put the colander?"

"It's under the sink, on a hook."

Graham opened the cabinet and felt inside until he found what he was looking for. "I kind of like the idea of being a research assistant," he said. "It would give me some time outside of school to see what it's like to work in academia. Maybe Dr. Blake would hire me. But he's gonna retire soon."

"Isn't that what he said freshman year?" Gina asked as she folded the napkins into shapes. "He said two years. I think he's still saying two years."

Graham shrugged and then picked up the large pot of pasta. He poured it out into the colander sitting in the sink. The steam rose up into his eyes, and he closed them briefly. "Yeah, and he's tenured. He could stay forever."

"It's an idea," Gina said. "There are other professors who might hire you, or you can work for a different company. Maybe one that makes neuroleptic medications."

Graham shook the colander until it stopped dripping and poured the linguini into a ceramic bowl. "I don't know if I want to sell out to Big Pharma," he said. "But again, it's something to think about."

"What time did Kaya say she and Gray were going to get here?"

Graham winced. "Don't call him Gray to his face," he said. "I tried it once. Kaya gave me an earful. They're coming separately. Kaya's coming straight from class. They should be here soon."

"Good," Gina said. "The sauce smells so good. I'm starving."

"I think Kaya and I should call our mom together while they're here," Graham said. He blew on a wooden spoon filled with sauce and then tasted it. "Maybe I *should* go to culinary school. I make a damn good tomato sauce."

"So does Mr. Ragu," Gina said, grabbing the jar and rinsing it out in the sink. "I think it's a good idea that you call your mom. I'd love to hear how her date went."

Graham put the spoon down on the counter. "I don't know if I want to hear about the date," he said. "I can't believe she went out with my childhood dentist. Did I tell you he used to keep hamsters in his waiting room? I bet they had the best hamster teeth in all of history."

Gina laughed.

A knock sounded on the door, and Gina opened it a few seconds later. "Oh, hi, Grayson," she said. "Come in."

"I brought some wine," Grayson said, handing a brown paper bag to Gina. "I had to have the RA on my floor buy it for me. I'm just glad campus police didn't stop me walking over here."

Gina smiled. "Take off your jacket. How was your day?"

"Great," Grayson said. "I had chemistry class today. I didn't think I'd like it, but I do, and I'm doing pretty well in it. I never really liked biology, but this stuff is much more interesting."

"That's great," Graham said, walking over and shaking his hand. "Welcome to our apartment. Have a seat."

Grayson helped himself to a seat on the couch. "I like it here," he said. "It's pretty close to campus. How did you get in here anyway?"

"It's a lottery," Gina explained. "Both Graham and I put our names in at the end of sophomore year. You have to be a junior to live here unless you're married. Graham's name got pulled. He was allowed to have whatever roommates he wanted, and he chose me. It's nice, because we turned the second bedroom into a study room. It's a good way to get space from each other to do our work if we need it, and if we don't, we just study down here."

"Good plan," Grayson said. "Maybe if things keep going as well as they are, Kaya and I can get a place in two years."

Graham gave him the side eye. "Two bedrooms," he said. "One for each of you." He laughed, and Grayson laughed with him.

"When does Kaya's class end?" Gina asked, handing Grayson a glass of the wine he brought.

"Five forty-five," Grayson said.

"It's six," Graham said. "She should be here in a few minutes."

"It's probably about a ten-minute walk," Grayson said. "Sometimes she talks to other people in her class after. She's trying to make friends outside our dorm. She'll be here in about ten minutes, I bet."

Gina sat down next to Grayson while Graham chopped vegetables for a salad. They all talked about their classes and going home for Thanksgiving. Graham brought the bowls with salad and pasta to the table and poured a glass of wine for Kaya.

"It's six fifteen," he said. "Shouldn't Kaya be here by now?"

Grayson took out his phone and looked at the time. His forehead wrinkled. "I'll give her a quick call."

He pushed a button on his phone and held it to his ear. Ten seconds later, he looked up. "I got her voicemail." He waited several moments and then spoke into the phone. "Hey, Ky. We're all waiting for you over here. You'll probably be here before I finish this message. Listen, call me as soon as you get this message to let me know when we should expect you. Love you babe. Bye." He hung up. "That was weird. She should have picked up."

Graham got a sick feeling in his stomach. "Do you think something's wrong? She should be here. Should we take a walk back that way to see if we run into her?"

Gina put her hand on his shoulder. "If you want to," she said. "I would say we should wait a minute or two, and give her a chance to get here. You know she wants you to trust her."

Graham knew she was right. Kaya was fine. He nodded. "Five minutes."

Five minutes went by without Kaya arriving. Grayson stood. "I think we should go find her. Maybe she stopped back in her room or something. Maybe her phone battery's dead and she didn't have her charger." He grabbed his jacket.

Graham started walking toward the chair where his jacket rested, but before he reached it, his phone rang. He dove for the table and picked it up. "Kaya?"

"Is this Graham Reed?" a voice said.

Graham's blood felt cold. "Yes," he said. He made eye contact with Gina, and she immediately picked up on the fear in his eyes.

"Mr. Reed," the male voice said. "My name is Sergeant Morris, from the campus police. Are you the brother of Kaya Reed?"

"Yes," Graham said quickly. "Is something wrong? Is she okay?"

Suddenly, Grayson was at his side, his hand grasping Graham's forearm.

"Mr. Reed, I'm afraid there's been an incident on campus involving Ms. Reed, and we could use your assistance."

"My assistance?" Graham asked. "What kind of assistance?"

"We have an ambulance coming to take Ms. Reed to the emergency room," Sergeant Reed said. "We need you to come down to our office and give us a bit of information, some history."

"Wait," Graham said, holding his hand up. "Is Kaya okay? Is she hurt?"

"Mr. Reed, as I said, Ms. Reed was involved in an incident. She isn't hurt."

"Then why are you bringing her to the hospital?" Graham pleaded.

"Because," Sergeant Reed said, "Ms. Reed appears to be going through a mental health crisis, Mr. Reed. She became hysterical on the quad and could not be calmed or redirected. It took two officers to restrain her enough to keep her safe from harming herself or someone else. Mr. Reed, your sister is being put on a mental health hold. She will most likely be admitted to the psychiatric unit this evening."

IT HAD BEEN A LONG, tiring day, and Kaya was looking forward to the end of class so she could walk to her brother's apartment for dinner. Grayson had promised to get hold of a bottle of wine. Kaya could use a glass of wine. Freshman year was supposed to be a year of discovery, but it had been a lot harder than she had expected.

In high school, she had been able to do all of her work, do it well, and go to cheer practice every day and hang out with her friends. Kaya loved cheerleading, and college cheer was even more amazing than she had expected. She was learning new things every day and becoming a much better dancer. She was in the best shape of her life. She had even taken to running for exercise early each morning to get fitter. She felt strong and in control of her body. The only thing she didn't feel strong about was her schoolwork.

The work wasn't exactly hard; she was just having trouble staying focused. And the class sizes were so large. She was always nervous being around dozens of other students during the lectures. She didn't always hear the voices, but sometimes, especially on Mondays, the voices were loud and distracting. She didn't dare tell Graham. She was trying to push through it. She had to figure out a way to deal with it. She wanted to make college work for her.

The professor finally ended the lecture, and Kaya stood up. The class had run late, and she needed to make her way to Graham and Gina's place. She put her books in her backpack and rushed to the door. It was getting dark outside. It got darker and darker every night, but Kaya wasn't scared. She was used to walking around campus late at night now. She liked to go to the library after dinner. Sometimes, she went with Grayson, and sometimes she went alone. When she was done, she walked home. If it got too late, Grayson insisted that she take the campus shuttle back to her dorm. He was worried about her safety, and she wanted to ease his mind. Besides, it was nice to get a free ride. It was a long walk.

There were other students walking in the same direction, but the farther she got from campus, the thinner the crowd became. Kaya was glad. It was nice to be close to alone in the quiet night. She looked up at the sky and saw the first stars of the evening emerging. She even made a wish on the first one she saw. She chuckled to herself. She knew that stars were just balls of gas out in the universe, but still, she wished out of habit. She continued to look up at the sky. The moon was rising, and it was a crescent. She liked that phase the best. It made her think of the man in the moon. She could picture him sitting atop the swoop, lounging, staring at the stars.

She was looking for Orion so she could find the Big Dipper when she ran into what felt like a padded wall and she fell backward. Her butt hit the pavement, and her backpack fell to the sidewalk. Her belongings scattered. She forced herself into a crouch and started to pick up her things.

"Let me help you," a voice called out. She looked up. A large man with a clean-shaven face and dark brown hair was standing over her. He must have been what she walked into when she was stargazing.

"Oh," Kaya said, still feeling a sense of shock from falling. "Okay. Yeah, thanks. Sorry about running into you like that."

The man reached out his hand, and Kaya took it. He started to pull her up. "It's okay," he said with a smile. "I probably wasn't paying attention anyway. . . . I want to drag you out behind this building, behind the dumpster, and I want to fuck your brains out from behind, whether you want me to or not."

Kaya gasped. "What?" she asked, horrified.

The man narrowed his brow. "I said it was probably my fault too," he said. "And you'll love every minute of it, bitch, if you make it out of there alive.'"

Kaya quickly pulled her hand away, fell backward, and screamed at the top of her lungs.

Chapter 12

Campus Police Report #32465
October 27, 2003

Subject: Kaya Reed, 18
Victim: Ted Stratton, 20

Critical Event: Per multiple witness reports, Subject was traveling east on foot near 244 NE Maple Lane. Victim was traveling west on the same road. Subject and Victim collided on the sidewalk, knocking Subject to the ground, scattering her books. Victim reached down to assist the Subject with standing, and Subject accepted the assistance by taking his hand. Seconds later, Subject let go of Victim's hand, and fell back to the ground. At that time, she screamed loudly, and began yelling at the victim, telling him to stay away from her. Subject then got herself to her feet, and ran at the victim, beating at him with her fists. Victim attempted to restrain the subject with his hands, at which time the Subject screamed again and yelled for help. Witnesses intervened at that time, and pulled the Subject away from the Victim. Victim sustained superficial scratches to his face and hands while trying to restrain Subject. Bystanders restrained Subject until Campus Police in the area responded and took control of Subject. It was necessary for two officers to subdue Subject with restraint and calming voices. Eventually, the officers were able to subdue Subject, at which time, Emergency Transport arrived at the scene. Officer Morris completed paperwork to have the Subject transported on police hold to Palmetto General Hospital for psychological evaluation. Charges are pending.

Signed:
Officer Douglas Morris, Sergeant, Campus Police, Badge Number 1534

Graham looked up, shaking his head. "No. Something's wrong here. This doesn't sound like Kaya at all. She wouldn't have done this. This guy, this Ted guy, he must have said something to her that upset her."

Sergeant Morris shook his head. "No, Mr. Reed," he said. "There were several witnesses at the scene. Many of them stopped to help after the collision, and they saw the whole scene. Mr. Stratton didn't say a word besides offering to help Ms. Reed up. He just put out his hand, she took it, and then she started screaming."

"Maybe he whispered something under his breath," Graham insisted.

"No, Mr. Reed," Sergeant Morris said. "There were two witnesses close enough to hear. They were bending down to help retrieve Ms. Reed's scattered belongings. Mr. Reed, the report you read is totally accurate. Your sister was unprovoked. She attacked Mr. Stratton for no reason."

"I don't understand," Graham said. "She's never done anything like this before."

"She has no history of mental illness?" Sergeant Morris asked, his pen poised over his notepad.

Graham hesitated. He had to tell the truth. "No, actually, Kaya does have a history of some mental health issues. Since she was fourteen, she's heard voices in her head. But they've always been so benign. They're just like thoughts that she thinks the other person was having. She's never had any voices tell her to do anything, or insult her, or threaten her."

He recalled when he found out that Kaya thought that Jill wanted her to die in cheerleading practice, the first time he had heard any sign of her voices, but he chose not to mention that now. Back then, Kaya hadn't reacted anything like this officer was describing. She had been calm and collected.

"No, she's been able to live her life with no problems at all. She's a really popular girl, really smart and funny, and she's on the University cheerleading team."

Sergeant Morris shook his head. "Well, it seems like maybe something's changed. Maybe she's experiencing new symptoms. Do you know if she had her medication adjusted recently?"

"Kaya's not taking medication," Graham said. "She's never needed it. Like I told you, the voices have never interfered with her life at all."

"Well, you can't say that anymore, Mr. Reed." Sergeant Morris jotted a note on his pad. "She could be facing charges of assault. And some of the things she told us about Mr. Stratton . . ."

"What did she say?"

"Well, she made some accusations against him," the officer stated. "She was calling him a predator, and a rapist. Pretty strong words. She tried to harm him. She said she needed to stop him."

Graham had been pacing with the police report, but after hearing all of this, he fell into the chair next to Sergeant Morris's desk.

"Oh my God," he said, putting his hand to his forehead. "I have to get to her. She must be so scared."

Sergeant Morris nodded. "I think that would be okay, but you should call over there first to make sure they'll let you see her. It might take some time to get her admitted. Things move very slowly in the emergency department. And if they don't have any beds there, they might have to transfer her to another facility."

"Facility?" Graham asked.

"Yes, there are a couple of free-standing psychiatric facilities in the Tri-County area. They take the overflow from the hospital. They don't have any medical treatment, so the whole place is focused on mental health. Most of them also have drug and alcohol treatment, which actually brings me to my next question. Does your sister typically drink alcohol, or use street drugs?"

"Street drugs?" Graham sat up straight. "Not that I know of. She never has more than a glass of wine at dinner sometimes. She doesn't like to drink because she's worried that it might, well, that it might change the nature of her voices. But she was coming directly from campus. She had a class. She wouldn't have had anything to drink."

"I didn't detect any odor of alcohol on her breath while we were restraining her. But they'll test her for any substances in her system in the emergency room."

"It will come out negative," Graham said.

"Then we'll have nothing to worry about," Sergeant Morris said. He closed his notepad. "Why don't you go out to the waiting area now. I'd like to have a word with Ms. Reed's boyfriend, Mr. . . ."

"Grayson," Graham said. "That's his first name. You know, I'm not sure of his last name. I've always just known him as Grayson."

Sergeant Morris nodded. "If you need to make any phone calls, you can use the phone in the waiting area. You need to dial nine for an outside call, and if you need to call long distance, you'll need to call collect. Maybe you'd like to call your parents."

Graham nodded and stood. He put his hand out and shook the officer's hand. "Thank you so much for getting in touch with me," he said. "I'm glad my number was in her school file for a local contact. Let me know if we need to get a lawyer or anything for Kaya."

Sergeant Morris handed a card to Graham. "It's been my pleasure, Mr. Reed. Call me if you have any other information, or any questions."

Graham went out to the waiting area while Grayson went back with the police officer. He took a seat next to Gina. He put his elbows on his knees and rested his forehead in his hands.

"This is unbelievable."

Gina put her hand on his back. "What happened?"

Graham told Gina everything. "And she might end up getting charged. Gina, something's wrong here. Kaya must have felt really threatened by this guy to react like that. I feel like he must have said something to her, or she recognized him or something."

"But she reached for his hand," Gina said. "It wasn't until then that she freaked out. She wasn't feeling threatened until then."

"But she got a good look at him," Graham said. He shook his head.

"At the beginning of the year, she told me that when she hears her voices, she thinks that they're controlled by things she picks up from the person whose voice she's hearing. Like, their facial expression, or their body language. It made so much sense to me. But this doesn't. The guy was trying to help her get up after knocking her over. Why would that set her off like that? The things she was yelling about were harsh. She said she needed to stop him. From what?" He shook his head again. "Maybe Sergeant Morris is right. Maybe her mental illness has gotten worse. Maybe she's seeing things going on where nothing is. Delusions. She's never seemed to have them before, but she's still young. And if she has delusions, that means that she has two symptoms of psychosis. That's not good, Gina. That means that she could have more at some point. God. I'll have to call my mother."

Gina rubbed his back in circles. "I'm so sorry, Graham," she said softly. "It's hard for me to believe, too. She's done so well for so long. Maybe your family just lucked out, and now some of that luck is gone. I really hope that the hospital can help her."

Graham looked up. "As soon as Grayson's done with the cop, I want to head over there. Morris said that they could end up sending her to another hospital if they don't have room, and I want to be there if that happens. I'm worried that if I'm not, no one will tell us where she ends up."

"Do you want me to come with you?"

Graham shook his head. "It's getting late. You can come if you want, but it will probably just be a lot of sitting around, waiting. I'm guessing Grayson will want to come. I don't think there'll be any talking him out of it."

Gina nodded. "You can just drop me off at home," she said. "I'll clean up from all the dinner prep. You guys have to make sure to get something to eat. You'll be no good to Kaya if you don't."

Ten minutes later, Grayson came out to the waiting area. "Let's go," he said, grabbing his jacket and walking toward the door. "We need to get to the hospital."

They dropped Gina off, and then Graham pointed his car in the direction of Palmetto Hospital.

"I can't believe this is happening," Grayson said, running his hand through his longish dark hair. "It's like this is a nightmare. How can this be Kaya? I mean, you know Kaya. She's . . . she's not crazy!"

Graham looked quickly at Grayson. "Did she ever tell you—"

"She did," Grayson said quickly. "She didn't tell me the truth at first. She was too scared. But then about a month later, she came clean and she told me about the voices. It kind of made sense when she told me. I guess she got lucky when she assumed what I was thinking when I met her. I really was thinking that. But I also must have looked like I was thinking it. It was a lucky guess. But I've never seen her get really upset, ever. I mean, she does get mad sometimes, like when we have a fight, but it's not irrational. She tells me, you know, when she hears them. Sometimes we laugh at them. But this . . . if she was hearing voices telling her things about this guy, she must have been terrified! She needs me. She needs us. They need to let us see her. But what if they don't?"

Graham shook his head. "I have no idea. The most important thing is that we know where she is so we don't lose track. Oh, God. I forgot. I need to call my mother."

He took his phone out of his jacket pocket.

"Can you call and put her on speaker? She'll probably want to drive out here. I don't want her driving in the middle of the night. She's in my call list under Mommy Dearest."

Grayson snickered then started to look through the phone. Graham heard it ringing, and then his mother answered.

"Mom," he said. "I'm in the car. We're all okay, but I have to tell you something. It's Kaya."

Mrs. Reed was already heading for her car by the time Graham and Grayson arrived at Palmetto Hospital. They rushed into the emergency room and headed right for the desk.

"I need to see my sister," Graham told the clerk. "Her name is Kaya Reed. They brought her in an ambulance."

The clerk checked his monitor and then his expression changed. "I'll have to have you take a seat," he said. "I'll call the social worker. She'll be out to see you in a few minutes."

Grayson was about to protest, but Graham grabbed his arm to stop him. They both walked over to the waiting area and fell into the plastic chairs.

"The social worker," Grayson said. "What if the social worker tells us to go away? Man, this is wild. We know her better than them. We should be in there with her, comforting her."

"We don't know what the social worker will say," Graham said. "Maybe they need to supervise our visit. They don't know us, or if we're safe to be around her. I mean, what if this Ted Stratton guy showed up and said he was her brother?"

Grayson lowered his head. "You're right."

They sat in silence, glancing at the news on the TV in the lobby. After fifteen minutes, the social worker arrived.

"My name is Mindy," she said. "I'm working with Kaya tonight. She's given permission for me to talk to her brother and her boyfriend. Come on in. There's a room for us to meet inside the main doors." She started to walk away.

Grayson ran up to her side. "Is she okay?" he asked. "She's not hurt or anything, is she? Has she been asking for me?"

Mindy looked at Grayson and smiled supportively. "We'll be in the room in a minute."

Grayson looked at Graham, his eyes pleading. Graham grabbed his arm again and directed him to keep following Mindy.

When they were seated and everyone was introduced, Mindy looked at them both with a kind expression. "Yes, Kaya has been asking for both of you since she got here. She's anxious to see you. You'll be allowed to see her in a while, but just briefly, and not alone. It's a hospital policy for safety. She's calm now, but still shaken up. She's had quite an ordeal tonight. She's exhausted, and the doctor ordered some medication to help to keep her calm. At least for a while. Right now, we're waiting to hear back from our community partners to see if there is a bed available to admit her tonight."

"Admit her?" Grayson asked. "Why? Why can't we just take her home? We can take care of her. She'd feel better if she was home. Or if she went to stay with Graham and his girlfriend for a couple of days. They could keep an eye on her."

Mindy shook her head. "At this point, there's no chance that Kaya will be discharged tonight. Dr. Kerr met with her earlier, and Kaya was terribly upset. She was very delusional, making comments about this man she encountered on the street tonight. She was going on and on about how he has to be stopped, and that no one else understands. She's going through a psychotic episode. She needs continued assessment and treatment. Kaya told me about her ongoing voices. They've obviously gotten worse. She needs to be kept safe until we can get them under control. Dr. Kerr has put her on a hospital hold for now."

Graham looked at Grayson, whose tears streamed openly down his face. Graham was trying to stay in control himself.

"What else did she say?" he asked Mindy. "Did she say what made her think that this guy was dangerous?"

Mindy thought for a moment. "I can give you a rundown of what she told me. She said that everything was going fine. She was going to your apartment from her class when she literally ran into this man. She fell over, and she felt silly. Her books were everywhere. She was about to collect them when he offered her his hand. She said she even smiled at him as she reached out, but then as soon as she touched his hand, he started saying things to her that scared her."

"What kinds of things?" Graham asked.

"I'm not going to tell you exactly what she said he said," Mindy told him, "but it was along the lines of him wanting to do things to her that were violent, in a sexual nature, and against her will. She was terrified. She felt she was in danger. That's when she started to scream. She said she tried to alert everyone else, to get them to grab him, but instead, they all ended up grabbing at her. She was confused, and kept trying to convince them."

"What about after the incident was over?" Graham asked.

"She said that it was clear to her that it was the voices," Mindy said, "but that it was different than anything she had ever experienced. She said that everything went from good to bad in just a split second. She felt that there was some kind of evil lingering around her. She told me that often she feels that her voices are based on real thoughts and observations. I've never heard of anything like that before. Graham, it's possible that her thoughts and feelings prior to today were based on delusions as well. I wonder if perhaps, well, if perhaps Kaya has become very adept at covering her symptoms."

"Covering?" Grayson asked. "You mean like lying about them?"

"Not really lying, no," Mindy said. "More like, disguising them, and not necessarily consciously. She has learned that telling others about what she's experiencing causes them distress and might lead to her being restricted from doing what she wants. So when she's around others, especially people who know her very well, she puts on a face like everything's fine. She appears to have convinced everyone around her that she's okay, but today, she was unable to do that. It was too much for her. She was stimulated by the voices, and she broke down. I'm afraid that if she doesn't get ongoing treatment, this type of thing will continue to happen, and every time it happens, it will become more real to her."

Graham sat stone still. He tried to process what Mindy had just told him. It couldn't be true. Was it possible that all of these years, Kaya had been pulling the wool over his eyes? His, and everyone else close to her? Could she have really been suffering in silence, not wanting anyone to know how deep it went? Now he felt his tears rising.

"I can't believe this," he said quietly. "I bought into it, hook, line, and sinker. All of this time, she could have been getting help. We could have been helping her, but she didn't let us."

"I don't think it was deliberate, Graham," Mindy said, placing a hand on his arm. "I think Kaya's not only been protecting you and your family, but also herself. It was too scary for her to admit that she was sick. It would have meant that she had to make changes in her life, changes she didn't want to make."

She looked briefly down at a paper on a clipboard on the table.

"Graham, Kaya says that there's no history of mental illness that she knows of in your family. Is there anything that you might know of?"

Graham thought about it. "Well, there's my dad. Something happened to him five years ago. Just out of the blue, he up and left us. All of us. He said he needed to get away and be by himself. Totally alone is what he said. He said it didn't have anything to do with my mother or us, and that he still loved us very much. He said it was just something he had to do. And then he left. He took almost nothing with him. He didn't even take his car.

He took a cab to the bus station. We haven't heard a word from him since. It's like he vanished off the face of the earth. My grandparents haven't heard from him either. Do you think it's possible that he had some mental health episode, too?"

Mindy shrugged. "It's possible. Usually psychosis presents itself to men when they're much younger, like Kaya's age. It *can* happen to older adults, but it's not as typical. But it is something to think about." She looked at the clock. "I think it's time to have you go in and talk to Kaya. I'm going to have you go one at a time, and security will be present. I do want to advise you both, though, not to try to challenge her beliefs too much. We'll do that in time, but right now, it's not the time. Just offer support to her, and love. Let her know that you accept her, no matter how she presents herself, mental health issues or none. And it's okay to be upset, and to cry, but please try to keep as calm as possible when talking to her." She glanced at Grayson. "She needs to know that the people she loves can help and protect her." Grayson nodded.

Graham went first. The door to the hold room was closed. The security officer opened it. Graham looked around before going in. Kaya was in the corner. The room was very small, the size of a closet. There was a chair that was basically a cushion to sit on, but Kaya had bypassed it in favor of sitting on the floor. There was a TV hanging from the ceiling, but it was not on. The rest of the room was completely empty. No magazines or pictures on the wall. Just a tiny room painted in a dull blue tone. Graham quickly went to his sister and got down on the floor with her. She looked sleepy, but when she looked up at him, she began to cry. She let herself fall into his arms.

"Are you okay, Ky?" Graham asked softly.

Kaya looked up at him. "Okay?" she asked. "How could I be okay? Graham, nothing's okay! It's all wrong. Everything. No one believes me! I know what I heard, Graham. You know what he said to me? I'll tell you. He said, 'I want to drag you out behind this building, behind the dumpster, and I want to fuck your brains out from behind, whether you want me to or not. And you'll love every minute of it, if you make it out of there alive.' Graham, that guy's a monster! No one did anything! They said *I* hurt *him*! He's gonna hurt someone, Graham, if he hasn't already."

"Kaya," he said, taking both of her hands, looking into her eyes.

Kaya's eyes went wide. She pulled her hands away from his.

"You don't believe me," she said, her voice turning raspy. "You're just like them! You think this is all mental illness! Graham! You of all people know that I don't lie. I don't make things up. I heard what I heard. And I told you before, yeah, they're voices, but they're based on what I see. I know it!"

She looked deeply into his eyes.

"I'm not hearing anything from you right now, Graham. You have to tell me."

She shuffled closer to him. Her eyes were pleading.

"Graham, please, tell me you believe me. Please!"

CHAPTER 13

DR. BLAKE PUT THE POLICE report down on his desk. "I'm so sorry," he said. "I know that Kaya was doing so well for so long. I'm sad to see that her symptoms are progressing."

Mrs. Reed dabbed at her eyes with a handkerchief she had been carrying with her for the last three days since arriving in Palmetto. "Dr. Blake," she said, "is there anything that you've discovered in the time that you've been meeting with Kaya that could be helpful? Something that we could share with the psychiatrist at Benson Hospital that could help them figure out the next steps?"

Dr. Blake sighed. "We've only met three times. We mostly talked about her history. She told me stories about things she had heard over the years, and her interpretation of what was happening at the time. We're booked to have time with the fMRI in January, so we haven't been able to get any data yet. But now I'm not so sure that's a good idea."

Graham's head jerked upright. "Why not? I mean, not many people with psychosis have the opportunity to participate in this kind of research.

I'd hate to see Kaya lose her opportunity to learn more about what's going on with her brain just because she had a bad episode."

Dr. Blake shook his head. "I'm not sure that I can ethically continue with this course of research, Reed," he said. "We were going on the premise that Kaya had something going on that had not been seen before. I'm not so sure that's the case now. It's possible that she was just in the early stages of her illness, and now it's starting to resemble something that has been through a lot of research."

He gave Graham a warm smile.

"I'll tell you what. I won't cancel our time with the fMRI just yet. I'll wait until Kaya gets fully assessed in the hospital and find out what the psychiatrist says. You said his name is Ernie Franklin? I've never heard that name before. But I'm not too familiar with the private, for-profit hospitals around here. I've mostly just worked with Palmetto."

"Dr. Franklin's the medical director and administrator of the place," Mrs. Reed said. "He says he has years of experience working with young patients like Kaya. I'm really hopeful that he can find a medication that works for her, one that she won't stop taking like she did last time. I really just want her to feel better, but I'm also concerned about her getting in trouble. The young man, Ted, has decided not to press charges against her due to the circumstances. I think that was the humane thing to do. He said he didn't want to draw all that negative attention to her while she's going through so much. I should probably send him a thank-you note or something."

"That would be nice," Dr. Blake said. "What can I do to help for now? Graham, I'd be willing to extend the due date of your final paper of the term if you need me to."

Graham shook his head. "No, I've pretty much got it done."

Dr. Blake shook his head. "Of course you do. It's not due for a month. I would expect no less from a student like you. However, if you need to take some time, and miss class, you would be excused. I know you'll make up any work you miss."

"Thanks, Dr. Blake," Graham said. "I might take you up on that."

"I can't believe I have to wait for visiting hours to see my own daughter," Mrs. Reed said in the car on the way to the hospital. "I should be able to see her whenever I want to, or she wants me to."

Graham pulled into the lot and looked around for a place to park. "I guess they have stuff they do during the day," he said. "You know, like therapy, and groups, and meals. They have a schedule. For a lot of the patients, the structure's really important."

"Kaya doesn't belong with those other people," Mrs. Reed insisted. "She needs to be home, with her family. We can help her there."

Graham pulled into a space, put the car in park, and looked at his mother. "I don't know. Mom, maybe this is the right place for Kaya. She needs to be around people who can help her. People who are trained to help her. We just see her as the great person she is. You know, funny, cute, talented—just Kaya. All these years, we've encouraged her, but have we really been helping her?"

Mrs. Reed looked at her hands in her lap. "I don't know, Graham."

Tears came back to her eyes, and her handkerchief came back out of her pocket.

"Do you think . . . do you think it's just gonna keep getting worse? Is Kaya going to have to leave college, and spend all of her time just trying to stay in reality? I can't accept that! There's too much life in that girl to just give up. But—but if she does give in to this illness, and we lose the person who she's been . . . I think of all she could lose. Her education, her cheering, her boyfriend, her future . . ." She trailed off and then blew her nose.

Graham felt waves of despair go through him, settling in his stomach. He had seen some of the other patients when he visited Kaya in the hospital the day before. Some of them seemed like they might be okay, but others wore what had seemed like vacant stares, and when they walked, it wasn't with grace and confidence like his sister. His sweet, enthusiastic sister, who had been sitting deflated on the holding room floor in the emergency department, and had been groggy and avoidant the day before when he tried to visit her at Benson Hospital. It killed him a little bit more inside every time he saw her.

"Let's just go in and see how things are today," he told his mother. "She has three days left on her hold, and hopefully she'll be well enough by then that she can be discharged. She can take a leave of absence, maybe, and go back with you to Wisteria and get some outpatient treatment. And then it's just a matter of waiting to see how she is."

Mrs. Reed nodded. She shoved her handkerchief in her pocket and opened the door.

"Okay, let's go," she said, stepping out of the car. Graham followed her to the entrance. "We're here for visiting hours," she told the receptionist. "Kaya Reed."

The receptionist had them sign in and sit in the lobby.

Five minutes later, a tech in blue scrubs came out to greet them. "I'll take you to her room," he said. "We tried to get her to come out to the day room, but she wouldn't go. I'm not sure how long she'll want you to stay. She really hasn't engaged with anyone all day." He left them at the door. "You have about an hour."

Mrs. Reed rapped softly on the open door. "Kaya? Kaya, Graham and I are gonna come in and visit you now."

She walked in and found Kaya sitting on the edge of the bed, her hands folded in her lap, her face blank.

"Kaya." She took her daughter's hand. "How are you?"

Kaya looked up slowly at her mother, her expression vacant. "You don't have to be scared to talk to me, Mom," she said dully. "It's still just me. And no, I'm not gonna do anything crazy while you're here."

"Kaya," Graham said, sitting on her other side. "No one's afraid of you doing anything while we're here."

"Mom is," Kaya said, looking at him. "She's afraid. She thinks I've changed, and she doesn't know me anymore. Do you feel the same way, Graham?"

Graham looked carefully at his sister. Her eyes had lost their shine. "I-I don't know, Kaya. It sounds like you hear Mom's voice telling you things about how she feels. But Kaya, isn't it possible that you're projecting your own feelings into her voice? Isn't it possible that you're feeling that you've changed, and you're the one who's scared?"

"I *am* scared, Graham," Mrs. Reed said. She turned to Kaya. "It's okay, Kaya. I don't mind if you know. I'm terrified. Just as terrified as I'd be if they told me you'd been diagnosed with cancer or some other disease. And I feel helpless. I'm not sure what I can do to help you, and it does scare me."

"You can believe me," Kaya said. "You can believe that I'm not crazy. I'm not homicidal, and I'm not just imagining the things that I felt from that guy that day. I'm not wrong, Mom. Graham. I'm right, but if I keep telling them that, they're gonna make me stay forever. But what can I do? No one believes me. So I have to wait until he hurts someone for everyone to believe me? No, just ignore the little schizo girl. She's just nuts!" She lay back on her bed, letting her head hit the pillow. "If you want to do something for me, get me out of here."

"Kaya," Graham said. "The guy who let us in here said that you're refusing to come out of your room. If you don't come out and do what they want you to do, they're not gonna think you're doing better. You have to do what you have to do to get out of here."

Kaya sat back up. "How on earth is an arts and crafts group gonna help me to not hear voices? Oh, and they had a group where everyone could process their emotions. What am I gonna do, tell them all that I was in a super good mood until the rapist knocked me down and told me scary things? How is that supposed to help?"

Mrs. Reed looked dangerously close to crying again. Graham made eye contact with her and hoped that his expression would tell her to try to hold it together.

"Kaya," she said, "even if you don't think it's gonna help, you have to do what they tell you. Are you taking the medication?"

Kaya rolled her eyes. "Did you know that on the first day I was here, they restrained me? They said I was fighting them. They said that I was a danger to others, and I had to take my medication. They didn't strap me down like they do in the movies, but they restrained me in a chair and gave me a shot." She laughed. "The nurse who gave it to me was thinking about her boyfriend the whole time. They'd had a fight the night before, and she wasn't sure if she was going to apologize, or wait for him to do it. There was a security guard, and he was trying to figure out where he was gonna go drinking with his friend after his shift. It was a great way to distract me while they shoved a needle in my ass. Man, at least they could have been thinking of something more entertaining."

Graham closed his eyes. "Kaya—"

Kaya shook her head. "You really think I've gone over the deep end, don't you?"

"Did you hear my voice say that?"

"No," Kaya said. "But I didn't need to. Your face says it all."

Graham sat silently. All of them sat silently. Graham didn't know what to say. He didn't think his sister was off the deep end, but at the same time, she couldn't be totally lucid.

"Kaya," he said softly. "I'm sorry my face looks like it does. Blame it on Dad. He's not here to defend himself."

Kaya stared at him in horror. But soon, her face softened, and she smiled. Then she laughed. "Oh my God, Graham," she said. "There's a time and a place for everything. This is the looney bin. No laughter allowed!" She sighed. "Seriously, though. I have to figure out how to get out of here. I think the way to do it is to just shut up about that guy. I just need to keep it to myself. If I stop talking about it, they'll think their stupid medications are working, and they'll spring me."

Mrs. Reed shook her head. "Kaya, no," she said. "You need to talk to them. You need to tell them everything. Baby, if this guy really is dangerous, there's no way to prove it anyway. But if he isn't—if it really is just a voice that's from your mind and not attached to him—then you really need help. Can you just consider that? It might be possible, even slightly, that your brain has started to manufacture voices that aren't so benign like they were before. Most people don't hear voices at all. You know that. It's not mainstream. You hear voices. Granted, they've been different than most. But they're still voices. It is, slightly, possible that your symptoms have gotten worse. It is possible that your mind is starting to believe them. It's possible that you're starting to fixate on them. Just, well, keep an open mind. Don't shut out the help you're being offered."

Kaya squinted at her mother for a few seconds. Then she opened her eyes wide. "Then I guess you don't want to hear about the voices I heard when I met the psychiatrist. What's his name? Dr. Jefferson?"

Graham smirked. "Dr. Franklin," he said. He was going to keep his mouth shut, but curiosity came over him. "What did his voice say?"

Mrs. Reed shot him a look. "Graham," she said. "Don't encourage it!"

Kaya laughed. "God, Mom. I'm not three, you know. I'm a grown woman." She turned to Graham. "He was thinking about all the money he could make from me with my private insurance. I guess most of the patients here are from the town, and they have Medicaid. They don't pay very much. But they can charge a lot more for private insurance and keep the patients longer. I guess he sees me as a money tree."

Graham bit his bottom lip. What Kaya was saying was true. Private institutions were able to charge more from private insurance. They preferred working with patients who had employer-paid insurance rather than those on public assistance. He had learned about all of this in one of his practical psych classes. He had no idea how Kaya knew about it. She was taking Psych 101, but there was no way they talked about insurance and reimbursement in that class.

"So you think this guy is driven by the all-American dollar?"

Kaya nodded. "Yeah," she said. "He said some other things, too, but I didn't understand them. I asked him about it, and he said he had no idea what I was talking about. I told him what his voice said, and he said that my voices aren't real. Then he decided to give me a higher dose of antipsychotics."

Mrs. Reed lowered her head. "Kaya," she whispered.

Kaya looked at her mother with concern and put her hand on her shoulder.

"Mom," she said softly. "Mom. I swear, it's gonna be all right. Okay? I just have to get through this. This isn't the end for me." She paused. "And I'm not gonna have to come live at home for the rest of my life, even if you want me to."

She pulled her hand back and placed it on Graham's arm.

"And you don't have to worry either," she said. "I won't have to drop out of school. I'm not gonna do anything stupid to get myself locked up in here forever, and I'm not gonna do anything to get myself arrested. I know it was a close call the other day, but the whole thing caught me off guard. I'll be more careful now, more discrete."

There was a knock on the door, and they all looked up.

"Good afternoon, Kaya," the man said, stepping into the room. He was wearing a long white lab coat over a shirt and tie. Graham noticed his expensive-looking shoes. "Hello everyone," he went on. "I met you the other day. I'm Dr. Franklin. I'm treating Kaya." He looked at Kaya and smiled. "Sorry to intrude upon your visit, but I was doing my rounds, and wanted to get a chance to check in on you. Kaya, I heard you haven't left your room all day. What's going on?"

Kaya shrugged. "I can't see any reason to leave my room," she said. "I'm happy here. This room has everything I need. There's a bed, and a window, and a lovely K-Mart painting of a girl and flowers over the bed. I notice it's bolted very strongly to the wall. And if I don't leave, they bring me my meals in bed. It's like being royalty."

Dr. Franklin shook his head lightly. "I'm glad to see you have a healthy sense of humor, Kaya," he said with a smile. "But I have to say, staying in your room all day is not going to help you get well. We'd like to see you get involved with our programming, interacting with staff and the other patients."

"Or," Kaya said, drawing out the word, "you could drop my hold and let me go home. I have classes to get to. And it's almost Halloween. Grayson and I were trying to come up with costumes to wear. I think it would be therapeutic for me to be able to go to a Halloween party like a normal college freshman and have fun with my friends."

Dr. Franklin's smile was pasted to his face. "Kaya, we'll talk more about this later." He turned to Mrs. Reed. "I would like to talk to you in my office for a moment." He turned to Graham. "You can join us as well. Kaya signed a waiver of confidentiality for both of you."

Graham looked at Kaya.

"What? Sure, you should both go into a different room and talk about my future. Sure. Just make sure when you're making plans to include me winning the lottery and moving to Los Angeles."

Mrs. Reed shot her a look and then turned back to Dr. Franklin. "Will we be able to come back and see Kaya before we leave?"

Dr. Franklin nodded, and Mrs. Reed nodded back. She and Graham followed the doctor out of the room and into an office. Dr. Franklin closed the door.

"Kaya's hold will be up in a couple of days," he said. "I wanted to let you know that I'm going to recommend to the court investigator that she go to court for a commitment hearing."

Graham's body jerked so hard that he almost fell forward out of his seat. "What?" he exclaimed. "Commitment? Kaya? Why? She's not a danger to herself or others. She had an episode, but it's over. She seems fine! Why on earth would anyone want to commit her?"

Dr. Franklin folded his hands in front of him on this desk. "Graham, is it? Graham, I've been noticing that Kaya's behavior adapts to who is with her at any time. When you or your mother are around, she is able to pull herself together and come across like she's okay, and that all of this is a mistake. But that's not the picture that we're getting of her here. I'm not sure if you're aware, but Kaya has made threats against the young man that she assaulted earlier this week. She has said that if released, she'll find him, and he'll regret his words. Need I remind you, the words she's referring to are auditory hallucinations. Kaya's been obsessed with the delusion that this man is dangerous, and she'll go to any length to stop him."

"Did she say anything specific as to what she'd do to him?" Graham asked.

Dr. Franklin shook his head. "Going to any length to stop him is close enough in my book. But there are other indicators that she's slipping into a delusional world. She has also made statements about me to me and my staff. She's convinced that I'm embedded in a conspiracy to defraud insurance companies, and that I'm cheating and billing for more than the services provided here. I can tell you quite clearly, that's not happening here. I would know." He chuckled. "And even if it was, how would an eighteen-year-old cheerleader from State find out? I don't mean to make light of this, but these are serious accusations. And her source? Her voices. She claims that she heard my voice telling her that I'm corrupt. I can assure you that I am not corrupt."

Mrs. Reed had her hand to her face. "So she's really suffering from delusions," she said. She shook her head. "She never had delusions before. Just the voices. The medication that you put her on, do you think it will help with the delusions?"

"That's the hope," Dr. Franklin said. "But I have to be truthful with you. There are different kinds of delusions. There's the kind that comes and goes and can be eased by medication. Then, there are fixed delusions. These are the ones that become a system of belief for the person, that work their way into their psyche, and become their reality. Medications can help keep these patients calm, but they can't take away the ideas."

"But Kaya just started having delusions," Mrs. Reed said. "It would seem that they would be the first kind, the kind that can be treated."

"We just don't know," Dr. Franklin said. "Kaya has just been discovered to have delusions, that's all. We have no idea how long she has been harboring similar delusions. Now that they are known, it's likely that she will continue to talk about them, and they will continue to develop. Look at how she has already added me to her delusional system. It's hard to say who will be next. We just have to hope that she can find some people, maybe some staff member here, or family or friends, that can support her and that she can trust. It's important for her to have someone she can trust."

"She can trust me," Graham said firmly.

Dr. Franklin looked at him. "I certainly hope so."

Graham folded his arms in front of him and shook his head. He grimaced.

"She doesn't need to be committed," he said. "I know about commitment. If she goes to court, the judge will throw the case away. She doesn't meet the criteria. She doesn't have a plan or means to 'stop this guy by any means.' She doesn't even know his name. I know you're gonna say it's public record, but we'll know if she tries to get access. I can tell you right now that if you release Kaya from the hospital, my mother will bring her back home, and I'll come with her, and we won't leave her alone for one minute. We know Kaya, and I know enough about mental illness to help her. I'm a psych major."

Dr. Franklin gave Graham a smug smile.

"I see," he said. "So you've been studying psych at State for a few years. When did you finish your medical degree, residency, and internship, and get twenty-two years of experience working as a psychiatrist? Once you've completed all of that, we can spend some time debating the merits of keeping a young girl with onset paranoid schizophrenia in the hospital for as long as it takes for her to become stable and be safe in the community. But for now, I'm going ahead with my recommendation. So if you'll excuse me, I have some paperwork to complete, and visiting hours will be over soon. I suggest you get back to Kaya right now if you want to wrap up your visit." He picked up his pen and started to write on a piece of paper.

Graham looked at his mother.

"I guess we've been dismissed," he said, standing. He walked to the door. As he stepped out of the office, he heard his mother apologize to Dr. Franklin for his outburst, and then she followed him out.

"Graham," she said, rushing to catch up with him. "Please. Don't alienate your sister's psychiatrist. This guy has the ability to help her get better and out of here sooner. Please. For me. Just chill out a bit, okay?"

Graham looked at his mother and then turned away and continued to Kaya's room. He walked in and smiled at his sister.

"So that guy's kind of a tool."

Kaya laughed. "My point exactly."

Graham looked at her intensely. "Kaya," he said softly. "They're gonna try to get you committed. Dr. Franklin's gonna recommend it to the county. Please, please promise me that you'll do everything they say. Please. You have to get out of here, and your attitude's not helping you. You have to play their game. I know you're not dangerous, Kaya. You have to stop telling them that you're gonna go after that guy."

Kaya looked confused. "What guy?"

Graham cocked his head. "The guy," he said. "The one you attacked."

Kaya shook her head. "I know what guy you're talking about, but I never said I was going after him."

Mrs. Reed pushed her way forward. "What?" she asked. "Dr. Franklin said that you told him that you'd do whatever it took to stop him."

Kaya scrunched up her nose. "I never said that. I mean, I would never stoop to his level. It's not in my nature to hurt people. Well, maybe when I feel like I'm unsafe, to protect myself, like I felt the other day, but I wouldn't seek him out. What I would do would be to go to the police and have *them* take care of him."

Graham and his mother looked at each other. "Kaya," Mrs. Reed said. "Dr. Franklin said that it seems that you're different around us than you are around everyone else. Maybe you want to protect us from how you really feel. Baby, I want you to be honest with us. If you've been telling people you want to get this guy, that's okay. I don't want you to hurt anyone, but I wouldn't be mad at you if that's how you felt."

Kaya shook her head furiously. "Mom, this is nonsense! I have not once made a threat to anyone! As a matter of fact, I was planning on talking to that Sergeant Morris once I got out of here to see if maybe there have been any complaints about this guy. Yeah, I know it was a voice I heard, but it felt very real to me. I think it could have been something I saw in his face. Graham, you know all about that. We've talked about it. He scared me. I just don't want to see him hurt anyone."

Graham got down on his knees in front of his sister and put his hands on either side of her face.

"Kaya," he said, looking right into her eyes. "Tell me right now that you're telling us the truth. Tell me right now. I can tell if I'm looking in your eyes if you're lying or not. Tell me. Now."

Kaya's eyes locked onto Graham, and she smiled. "Graham," she said. "I'm telling you the truth."

He kept his hands in place. "Kaya," he said softly. "I'm thinking of a number between one and ten. What is it?"

Kaya looked at him, and a smile spread across her face. "Three and a half," she answered confidently.

Graham's hands dropped quickly from her face. He caught his breath.

"I believe you," he said. "I have no idea why this guy is saying you said that stuff. Maybe he misunderstood. Maybe one of the staff got you mixed up with someone else. I don't know. But whatever it takes, we're gonna get you out of here, even if it means I have to testify at a commitment hearing."

A tech appeared at the door. "Visiting hours are over," she said. "I'm going to have to ask you to wrap it up."

Graham nodded to the tech before turning back to Kaya. "We'll be back tomorrow. We'll talk to the court representative and tell him that we support you getting discharged. We'll do what it takes."

Kaya smiled and nodded. "I know you will." She pulled him into a hug. "And by the way." She pulled away. "I really like the idea of me and Grayson being Patrick and SpongeBob for Halloween. Thanks for the suggestion."

She hugged her mother and said goodbye.

Graham and his mother walked to the exit and signed out.

Outside, the sky was growing dark in the mid-Autumn evening, and stray brown leaves were blowing around the parking lot in the soft wind. Graham opened his mother's door and then started to walk around the car to the driver's seat. He stopped short, Kaya's comment about Halloween playing in his head. He closed his eyes. His feet went numb.

Graham had not said anything to Kaya about what to wear for

Halloween. It had been a thought that popped into his mind while he was hugging her. He had thought that he would try to get Kaya out of the hospital before Halloween so she and Grayson could go to a party in a cute couple's costume, like Patrick and SpongeBob. He had never said it out loud, but somehow, Kaya had known.

"Oh my God," he said softly. He lowered himself until he was kneeling on the asphalt and pressed his head to his knees. "Oh my fucking God. Oh my God."

The number that Kaya had jokingly guessed had been three and a half. And that was the exact number that Graham had been thinking.

Chapter 14

"DR. BLAKE!" KAYA EXCLAIMED, RISING from her bed on weak legs. "What are you doing here?"

Dr. Blake welcomed Kaya's embrace. "Reed told me what happened," he said. "I came to check in on you, to make sure you're being treated well and such."

"It's Graham," Graham said. "Last name Reed."

"Very well, young man," Dr. Blake said. He sat on the bed, patting the mattress so Kaya would sit beside him.

Graham was blatantly aware of the fact that there were no chairs in the room. He wondered what a psychotic or suicidal person would do with a chair if they had the chance.

Dr. Blake took Kaya's hand. "Tell me, young lady, how are you holding up?"

Kaya's face went slack. "I want to go home," she said. "Either home. My dorm room or back to Wisteria. I don't even care which one. I want to go to dinner and a movie with Grayson. I want to take a shower using my own shampoo."

"Have you even taken a shower since you've been here?" Graham asked. "You're looking kind of ripe."

Kaya glared at him. She looked back at Dr. Blake. "You're the first person who totally believes me. I can hear it. You think I need to be released, and to be left alone to my own devices. Thank you for that."

Dr. Blake glanced at Graham and then back at Kaya. "Kaya," he said softly. "We need to talk about something."

Kaya nodded. "Something's changed. You think there's something going on that you don't understand." She looked at Graham. "That's what his voice is telling me, anyway."

She turned back to Dr. Blake.

"Maybe I'm just seeing that in your face."

"Kaya," Graham said, getting down on the floor in front of her and sitting cross legged. "We need to talk to you about something you said when I was here with Mom yesterday."

Kaya's eyes widened. "What was it? I said a lot of things."

"It was about Halloween."

Kaya laughed. "Brother, I'm stuck in a looney bin, and you want to talk about Halloween? You're weird. You wanted to talk about that yesterday too, remember? I thought that was bizarre, too."

Graham squinted at her. "Yesterday? You mean, you thought I said that out loud?"

Kaya's mouth opened slightly. "What? You didn't? That stuff about me and Grayson being able to have Halloween? I could have sworn you really said that."

Dr. Blake's forehead furrowed. "You didn't notice that his lips weren't moving at the time?"

Kaya shook her head. "We were hugging goodbye." She rolled her eyes. "Oh, for Christ's sake. Now I can't even tell the difference." She looked at her feet. "Maybe I am losing touch with reality."

Graham shook his head. "No, Kaya, you don't understand." He looked at Dr. Blake, and the professor nodded. "Kaya, when you said that, I didn't think anything of it either. It wasn't until I left and got to the car that it hit me. And now, I'm starting to second-guess everything that's happened in the last four years. I was up most of the night running it through my brain and I can't make any sense of it. That's why I asked Dr. Blake to come with me today."

Kaya shook her head. "Graham, you're not making any sense at all. What kept you up all night? Trying to decide what Halloween costumes you and Gina would wear this year?"

Graham chuckled despite the gravity of the conversation. Kaya was incorrigible. Even while locked in a psychiatric ward with the threat of commitment hanging over her head, she was making jokes.

"No, Kaya," he said with a small roll of his eyes. "Although if Halloween isn't canceled this year for us due to circumstances, I guess we have to start thinking about it. No. What kept me up is this: I didn't say anything out loud to you about SpongeBob and Patrick."

Kaya shrugged. "So maybe I made that up." She looked at her hands. "But it would be a weird thing for me to make up, seeing as I have no idea who Patrick is. I mean, I've heard of SpongeBob, of course, but I guess I just assumed that Patrick was another character in the show."

"That's just the thing, Kaya," Graham said. He took a slow breath and then blew it out. "I know who Patrick is. I watch SpongeBob sometimes on the weekend when Gina's sleeping in and I'm eating my cereal. It's funny. And I heard that it was gonna be a popular pairs costume this year."

"And?" Kaya asked, circling her hand to move him along.

"And," Graham went on. "And I was thinking that it would be a cute couple's costume for you and Grayson. You could be SpongeBob, and he could be Patrick."

"Okay?" Kaya said, still not picking up on what he was telling her.

"Kaya," Graham said quietly. "I was thinking that. Don't you see? I was *thinking* it when I was hugging you. But I didn't say it out loud."

Kaya stared at him. "You must have." She shook her head. "I wasn't looking at your face, and I couldn't have just pulled that thought out of thin air. Maybe you thought that you didn't say it, but you did."

"No. Like I said, it hit me after we left last night. When I got in the car, I asked Mom about it. I had to check myself. I knew I hadn't said it out loud, but I was second-guessing myself. But Mom swears I didn't say it. She was wondering what you were talking about when you were going on about it, and she was going to ask me about it. So she and I got to talking about it, and we talked for a long time. The things you said yesterday, about how Mom and I were feeling about you being in the hospital, and about your symptoms. Kaya, they were right on the nose. You seemed to know exactly how we were feeling, and it couldn't just be because you were looking at our faces. The more we thought about it, the more we realized that sometimes when you were telling us what the voices were saying to you yesterday, you were using some of the exact words from our own thoughts."

Dr. Blake nodded. "Kaya, you know that people don't really think in sentences most of the time, unless they're very focused on something in particular, or rehearsing something they want to say. Thoughts are fragmented, more like ideas, and images. But we associate them with words when we convey our thoughts to others."

Kaya nodded. "Okay," she said. "So what is it that you're both trying to say to me then?"

"Kaya," Graham said softly, reaching up to take her hand. "We're trying to say that there's more going on here than we originally thought. It seems that maybe, and I don't know how or why, but you're actually able to hear, or interpret, thoughts."

Kaya stared at him and then burst out laughing. "Oh my God," she said, shaking her head. "Guys, I'm the one on a five-day psychiatric hold, right? You two are supposed to be the voices, no pun intended, of reason. Now after four years of everyone telling me that I've been hallucinating the voices of people around me, you're trying to tell me that I'm not nuts at all, right? That I *am* hearing voices, but that I'm not making them up myself in my brain. Is that what you're saying?"

Graham thought carefully of how to go forward. "I don't know. I mean, there are a lot of coincidences. I've read enough in my life to know that after a while, if there are a lot of coincidences, they stop being coincidences, and we need to start looking for a connection."

He paused.

"For instance, the whole thing with Jill. You were always talking about her telling you all the bad things she wanted to do to you. I was worried about you, because I thought you were making it all up in your head at the time. That was before we really knew about the whole voices thing. But I can clearly remember you giving me the details of her wanting to put laxative in your milk. That's pretty specific, right? I thought your brain was being really creative with that one. But then later you told me that she tried to do the exact same thing to Bailey, and she was caught."

Kaya looked out the window, appearing to be deep in thought.

"I guess I kind of forgot about that," she said. "I got so wrapped up in the whole thing with the voices that I didn't even think about that. Yeah, that's kind of weird, huh? How come you didn't say anything back then?"

Graham shrugged. "I guess I just assumed that you had overheard something and you'd forgotten about it. But when you really think about it, would Jill have even said anything like that out loud?" He sighed. "But then I would have also had to accept that maybe all the things you said about Jill were true, that she thought about you being dead. And that was probably too much for my fragile little brain to handle."

He squeezed Kaya's hand.

"And now I have to come to terms with the fact that you might have been right. Jill might have been responsible for your fall from the pyramid. And if that's the case, Kaya, I can't even begin to apologize to you for not believing you."

Kaya's eyes were open quite wide as she stared at her hand in Graham's.

"You really believe all this," she said with disbelief. "You really think that I can tell what people are thinking." She looked into his eyes. "Just now, I could hear your voice telling me that you can't even begin to make it up to me, all the years that this has been going on, and you doubted me. That you might have contributed to me doubting myself."

Graham nodded. "That's exactly what I'm thinking." He smiled slightly. "Like Dr. Blake said, it's more like a conglomeration of thoughts, but when you say it, it's like you take the words right out of my head. If I was going to describe my thoughts, that's how I would describe them."

Kaya sat for a long time in silence. The two men sat silently with her. Finally, Kaya freed her hand from Graham's grasp and stood. She started to pace the room.

"Oh my God," she said softly. "I feel like now I have to go back, all the way back for the whole four years and review everything. Everything I heard, and see it in a new way."

She fingered the frame of the picture over her bed.

"Everything. I have to come to terms with the fact that I've been seeing all of this wrong."

She turned back to Graham. "So Grayson, when he said, 'Wow' . . ."

Graham smiled. "He was really saying, 'Wow,'" he said.

Kaya nodded, her eyes fixed on a spot on the blank wall.

"And when Jill said she wanted me dead . . ." She shivered. "I'm not sure that Jill did cause the fall," she said. "I think—I think she said something. Something like, 'I'm really gonna do it this time,' and I heard it, and I yelled, and I panicked, and I lost my balance."

She shook her head.

"So in a way, it was a self-fulfilled prophecy, and she got what she wanted." She laughed. "But she didn't, because what she wanted was the top of the pyramid, and Miss Green gave that to Bailey."

She sat back down.

"So that also means that the guy, the one I ran into the other day—what's his name?"

Graham hesitated, but then remembered that his sister wasn't a homicidal maniac after all. "Ted Stratton."

Kaya nodded. "That means that what I heard him say . . ."

"It was true," Graham said, noticing that his voice sounded rough. His heart was pounding with the thought. The guy had really thought those things about Kaya. But would he have acted on them? "Kaya, they were his thoughts," he said. "He didn't say them out loud. It's possible he was thinking them but wouldn't have acted on them."

Kaya nodded automatically. "Do most guys have thoughts about raping women behind dumpsters, and then possibly leaving them for dead?"

Graham felt chills down his spine. "No," he admitted. "No. They don't. At least I hope they don't."

Dr. Blake shifted on the bed.

"Kaya," he said. "I think we need to talk a little more about the functionality of your, well, gift, I guess we can call it. It seems that these voices, or thoughts, that you hear only happen sometimes, from what you've told me."

"Right," Kaya said. "They only happen when I'm close to someone. Like standing near them. And I only hear one voice at a time." She thought about it. "Yeah, I guess that's true. I could be in a classroom with thirty other students, but only hear my friend Bailey singing."

She laughed.

"Oh my God. That means that Bailey was really only singing in her head all this time, not out loud! That's hysterical." She paused. "Or maybe not. Maybe it's really distracting to hear music in your head all the time."

"I would think that it would be distracting for you to hear voices in your head," Dr. Blake said. "But it doesn't seem that it is. You seem to be selective in what you hear. So you have some sort of focus. I wonder what causes you to focus on one person when several are in the room."

Kaya shrugged. "I have no idea. I would think maybe it would have something to do with them being people I know, but sometimes it would happen in the lunch line in high school, and some of the kids I didn't even know."

Dr. Blake scratched his balding head. "Okay, so this is a quandary. Let's take it case by case. What's the first voice you ever remember hearing?"

Kaya's eyes turned up toward the ceiling. "I'm not entirely sure," she said. "For a long time, I just thought people were saying weird things to me, and I didn't know they were voices."

Her mouth clamped shut.

"Wait. I do remember something that was weird."

She thought for a moment.

"It was a few months before everything started with Jill. No, wait. It was longer than that."

She turned to Graham.

"It was before Dad left. Something had happened that day, I don't remember what, but I was upset. Something at school. I think maybe Cat had said something that upset me. I was talking to Dad about it, and he was comforting me. Then suddenly he said something weird. What was it? It was something like, 'I wish I could take all of your pain away. If I could make it different for you, I would. But I just don't have control over it.' I remember thinking it was a strange thing to say, so I questioned him about it."

Graham felt cold. "What did you say to him?"

Kaya closed her eyes in thought. "I said 'control over what?' And then he pulled away and gave me this scary look. Like he was scared. I'd never seen him look like that before. But then he smiled and said it was nothing. I forgot about it pretty quickly."

Dr. Blake nodded. "So at the time, you thought he had said that out loud to you. Why didn't you notice that his lips weren't moving?"

Kaya thought and then shrugged. "He was hugging me. I couldn't see his lips."

Dr. Blake nodded again. "Okay. Now let's go forward to the events with the cheerleader girl. You heard her make threats to you, but again, you didn't notice that her lips weren't moving."

Kaya nodded. "We were in pyramid formation. She was on the second tier, and I was on her back. Her head was pointed away from me. I thought it was strange that she would say something so horrible in front of everyone."

Graham paid close attention to Kaya's words. "What about Bailey? Why couldn't you tell that her lips weren't moving?"

"She was sitting behind me," Kaya said. "Remember I told you the classroom was really crowded? We were all right on top of each other. Sometimes, her legs were stretched out under the desk and her feet were touching mine." She laughed. "Sometimes we would actually foot wrestle under the desk!"

Graham felt the anticipation of a breakthrough coming. "What about Cat?" he asked. "Remember that time in your room when you said that she told me she loved me right in front of me?"

Kaya nodded. "Yeah," she said. She smiled. "I guess she really did! But let me see. We were in my room, practicing cheers. We were next to each other. You came into the room. I guess I just wasn't looking at her?"

Graham shook his head. "Maybe. You were both looking at me. But let me think for a second." He looked at the floor. "When I came into the room, you were showing her some steps. You were right next to each other. And you were holding hands."

Kaya nodded. "Yeah. I remember that cheer. It was called the chain."

Dr. Blake nodded, seeming to catch on to what Graham was getting at. "Kaya, I'd like to try something right now if that's okay with you. A small experiment."

Kaya nodded.

"I want you to look at me, look into my eyes. And I want you to concentrate and try to hear my thoughts."

Kaya looked at Dr. Blake. "I've never done it like this before," she said. "I'm not sure if there's something I need to do to make it happen."

She sat quietly for several seconds. Then she shook her head. "No, I'm sorry. I've got nothing. I guess I can't just make it happen."

Dr. Blake reached out and put his hand on her arm. "That's okay, Kaya. You can try again later."

Kaya suddenly looked up at Dr. Blake. "Oh my God," she said in a whisper. "Yes."

Graham tilted his head. "What just happened?"

Dr. Blake smiled. "I just thought something toward Kaya. I told her that if she could hear my thoughts, to say yes out loud. I did that before, too, but it didn't work."

Kaya shook her head. "What's the difference?"

Dr. Blake looked at Graham. "Now you try, Reed."

Graham tried to send a thought toward Kaya. She shook her head after several seconds. "I'm not getting anything."

Dr. Blake nodded. "Now, Graham, take Kaya's hand."

Graham did as he was told and again directed a thought at his sister. She laughed and turned to Dr. Blake. "He said to tell you that it's Graham. Last name Reed."

Graham felt the light had just started shining into the room.

"It's touch," he said. "You have to be touching someone to know what they're thinking. You were hugging Dad. You were on Jill's back. You were holding hands with Cat."

He felt a dark wave come over him. "And Ted Stratton was pulling you up by your hand."

Kaya nodded. "That makes so much sense. Bailey's foot touching my foot. Grayson touching me in the lunch line when we both reached for the same pudding."

She turned toward Dr. Blake. "They want to commit me. If I tell them that I can read minds, that will seal the deal! How can I convince them that I'm not crazy?"

They all sat with that thought for a while and then something occurred to Graham.

"Kaya, you told me that when you met Dr. Franklin, you got bad vibes off of him about your insurance. And then there was some other stuff that you heard, but you didn't go into detail. You said that you told him about it, and he played it off like you were crazy. What exactly was it that you heard?"

Kaya thought about it. "It was really brief, because he was shaking my hand after he introduced himself to me. First I could just tell that he was chomping at the bit to assess me and find a reason to keep me here because my insurance is so good. But then I picked up quick bits and pieces of stuff about Medicare. Huh. Medicare. That should have been my first clue that I was reading his mind. I know nothing about Medicare. He was thinking about some paperwork, and having to get it done, and how he could do it convincingly. Something about reconciling the books or something."

Graham nodded. "And you told him what you heard?"

Kaya nodded.

"And if you were reading his mind . . ."

Realization came to Kaya's eyes. "Then he would see me as a threat," she said. "I know his dirty little secret. So if I'm really, really crazy, no one will believe me."

"And if he keeps you in the hospital, he can continue to document how crazy you are," Graham went on. "Crazy enough to threaten some poor innocent boy on campus for no reason."

"Crazy enough to be committed," Kaya said. "The girl who got committed for hearing voices that were bad enough to drive her to violence. Who would believe that girl when she started to talk about the hospital administrator committing fraud? It's just another part of her delusional system."

Dr. Blake smiled. "Maybe this is your ticket out of here," he said. "I don't want you to do anything that makes you feel uncomfortable, Kaya, or could put you in danger, but how would you feel about possibly laying hands on Dr. Franklin one more time?"

Chapter 15

"SO YOU KNOW THERE ARE cameras in every room," Kaya said as they sat around in a huddle, she and Dr. Bishop still on the bed, and Graham on the floor. "I don't know if they look at them all the time, but they can at any time. So I have to keep looking like I'm distressed." She put her hands over her face to demonstrate. "I'm pretty sure they don't have sound, so we're okay. But yeah, make sure to keep looking like you're concerned about me so no one gets suspicious."

She grabbed a tissue out of a box on the windowsill and dabbed at her dry eyes.

"So what do you think I should do?"

Dr. Blake thought about it. "I'm not too sure. Somehow you need to get Dr. Franklin thinking about his fraud. You have to make him concerned enough to think about the details. Then you have to get enough details so that we can use them against him later. We have to decide what we want to do with the information. We can't pursue anything without solid evidence, and mind reading doesn't hold up in court, just as Dr. Franklin told Graham and your mother. But even so, if you put the idea of fraud out there to the world, people will start thinking about it, and maybe they already suspected it. Then maybe someone investigates. But then there's the other issue. It's possible, and likely, that Dr. Franklin is keeping Kaya in the hospital until he can discredit her enough so he feels safe. We could use the information that Kaya gets for leverage to get her discharged, and to avoid the whole commitment process. But if we do that, we might not be able to get him investigated."

Graham shook his head. "I wish there was a way to do both. It's not fair to Kaya to be in here. I mean, a psychiatric hospital is the right place to be if someone really needs it, don't get me wrong. But there's nothing wrong with Kaya."

He grinned at her like only a brother can grin at a sister.

"At least not when it comes to hearing voices!"

Kaya sneered. "There's a time and a place, Graham," she said. "And I know you are, but what am I?" She covered her face again and laughed.

Anyone looking at the surveillance at that moment could have mistaken it for sobbing.

Graham put his hand on her knee in a gesture that could represent support. Then he thought *I'm rubber and you're glue*, and Kaya laughed again.

Dr. Blake rolled his eyes. "Just because we know what Kaya can do now doesn't mean you can use it secretly when there are others in the room. That's a bit rude."

Graham kept himself from smiling for the camera. For the past half hour, he felt like four years of heavy weights had been lifted from his shoulders. He had his sister back. She was going to be okay. He didn't understand what was going on with her, and how she was able to hear thoughts, but he didn't care. She wasn't sick, and she wouldn't be getting worse as he and his mother had feared.

Mrs. Reed was back at her hotel at the moment, doing whatever she could to distract herself while her son and Dr. Blake talked to Kaya. She hadn't been sure what to believe, but she was trying to keep an open mind. She wanted more than anything to believe that Kaya would be okay, even if it meant that she had to suspend disbelief for it to be true. He was looking forward to getting back to her to let her know what they had learned, but he wished that he would be able to bring Kaya with him for that conversation.

It seemed appropriate for her to be there. And aside from that, he had some other questions for her. Questions about their father.

"So I'm supposed to meet with Dr. Franklin this afternoon," Kaya went on. "It's our regular meeting to discuss how things are going with my medication."

"Are you taking them?" Graham asked.

Kaya nodded. "I have no choice," she said. "They check your mouth after they give them to you. If you're on a hold or committed, they can decide to give you a shot if you refuse your medication. It's not so bad. Obviously, it doesn't stop my voices. It makes me tired, and my mouth is always dry. But as soon as I get out of here, I'm done with them. I just hope I never end up back in a place like this. If I do, I'll probably have to take them again."

"You're not gonna end up back in a place like this," Graham promised. "What happened was a fluke. You were terrified. But you know more now. If God forbid something like that happens again, you'll just keep your mouth shut, and then when it passes, you'll do what you can to follow up on it. I mean, this thing with Ted Stratton isn't over, Kaya. The guy is dangerous. If he thought that stuff about you in a split second like that, chances are he's thought it before, and maybe even acted on it."

Kaya shivered, not having to act for the camera. "I have to figure out how to take what I know from the thoughts I hear and then maybe find evidence to support it. If I go to the police with some story about hearing thoughts, I'll be back through this door before I say another word."

"Which brings us back to Dr. Franklin," Dr. Blake said, trying to refocus their attention. "So you'll meet with him this afternoon, and somehow you'll bring up the fraud issue again. And then you have to find a way to make physical contact with him."

Kaya grimaced. "Gross," she murmured.

Graham shook his head. "Why do I feel like I'm in the Scooby Doo gang all of the sudden?" he asked. "At the end of all this, are we gonna pull off Dr. Franklin's mask to reveal who he really is?"

"The devil," Kaya said. "I mean, who else would take advantage of a bunch of vulnerable people suffering from mental illnesses? He's a piece of shit, and he deserves to lose his license, and even go to prison."

Dr. Blake nodded. "He's the worst kind of criminal," he agreed. "The kind that gains your trust and makes you think they're helping you. So let's think of how you can make contact."

Kaya thought about it. "I could thank him for all of his help. I could play grateful for him trying to help me get better, and looking out for me. I could shake his hand, and then hold on, and put my other hand over his while I lay on the crap about him bringing me to the light. I was so buried in denial before I came to the hospital, and now I have awareness, blah blah blah. I could probably keep that up for a good thirty seconds. That might be enough."

"Do you think you could say all that without barfing?" Graham asked.

Kaya side-eyed him. "I'm a cheerleader, Graham," she explained. "Do you really think I believe the team is going to come back and win after being down forty-seven points? No. I know how to bullshit. It's part of the job."

"Okay," Dr. Blake said. "So you'll meet with him, get him talking about your voices telling you about his fraud, and how you realize now that they were just voices and not true. Then you'll thank him, and maintain contact for as long as you can to read his thoughts. Then you'll get out of there."

Kaya nodded. "But then what?"

"I've been thinking about that," Dr. Blake said. "Then, I request a meeting with Dr. Franklin. Colleague to colleague. And he and I will have a talk. It would be even better if Graham were there as a witness. Yes. I think that's what we'll do. I can even say it's part of his psych training. He's my research assistant. Yes. I'll tell him about the times I've met with Kaya, and that maybe I can offer some insight. And then, when his guard is down, I'll tell him what we know."

"But will that work?" Graham asked. "Like we've been saying, it's all conjecture. It's all from the brain of someone who is known to have a psychotic disorder." He looked at Kaya. "At least allegedly. How can we make this work?"

Dr. Blake gave a small smile. "No one gets away with Medicare fraud for long periods of time. Somehow, they mess up and get caught. Now, our Dr. Franklin knows that Kaya knows something, but he doesn't understand how she knows. Maybe, just maybe, I've heard rumors before, and hearing

Kaya spout delusions about him made me think about what I heard. He has no idea what I've heard. He has a lot to lose, our doctor friend does. So he's likely to feel the pressure. Remember, I'm a tenured professor, and well known for my work. I may have never heard of Dr. Franklin, but I would bet dollars to donuts that he's heard of me. He might have even read my textbook in Intro to Psychology as an undergrad. I'm well respected, my dear children. He won't want to take the risk."

Graham felt hope growing within him. "So we tell him that he needs to discharge Kaya. Or what?"

Dr. Blake shrugged. "Or nothing. He just needs to discharge the girl. I make no promises. Let him think whatever he chooses."

Graham tried to hide his smile. He lowered his head and raised his hand to his face to block it from the camera. The plan was brilliant. They could have their cake and eat it too.

"I'm in," he said with confidence. He looked at Kaya.

"I'm totally in," she said. "I want to be home cuddling in bed with my Grayson by tomorrow night."

Graham grimaced. "Gross," he said. Then a thought hit him. "Oh my God. The things you must hear him think."

Kaya laughed. And she couldn't stop laughing. Anyone watching her monitor would have thought that she had become delirious.

"It's done," Kaya told Graham on the phone later that evening.

"What did he say?" Graham asked.

"I can't say," Kaya said, her voice low.

"Oh," Graham said. "You're in public. I get it. Did he implicate himself?"

"Oh, yeah," Kaya said. Graham could almost hear her smile. "And then some."

"Great. So we have to regroup and get the details. Dr. Blake will call in the morning to set up the appointment with Dr. Franklin. The only thing that worries me is that he won't have time tomorrow, and it's Friday. If you have to stay the weekend, Kaya—"

"I'll do what I have to do," Kaya said, but Graham could hear the strain in her voice. "We just have to do this. So have Dr. Blake ask to meet with me before the meeting, to check in on me, and tell them that you'll be there, too, and I'll give you the details. Then, you can go spring it on him."

"That's the idea," Graham said.

When he hung up the phone, he turned to his mother, who was sitting on the other bed in her hotel room with Gina and Grayson.

"The eagle has landed," he said.

Mrs. Reed shook her head. "I'm nervous about this. What if it backfires?"

"How?" Graham asked. "Dr. Franklin declares both me and Dr. Blake insane, and puts psychiatric holds on both of us? Mom, I think that would make people suspicious."

"People like Dr. Franklin don't have a conscience," Mrs. Reed went on. "You don't know how he'll react. What if he has a gun? What if he shoots both of you, and then says that he was defending himself?"

"You could let him know that other people know," Gina suggested. "That way, if he threatens you, he'd have to threaten them, too, and he doesn't know who they are."

"You could tell him that you have a letter written to the police," Grayson put in. "And if you don't survive the meeting, someone's been instructed to send it."

Graham laughed. "I really think that our society is inundated with police procedural series on TV," he said. "Those are classic moves. But they might work. I don't think Dr. Franklin will become violent. From what I've seen of him, he's a coward. He commits his crimes behind the scenes. Fraud is a coward's robbery. I'm not glorifying bank robbery, but his are true white-collar crimes."

"I'm starting a list," Mrs. Reed said quietly.

Gina turned around to look at her. "What kind of a list?"

"A list of people that I need to get back at for hurting my daughter," she said. "There's that Jill girl, and then this Ted Stratton, and Dr. Franklin. Anyone else I need to know about?"

Graham hesitated before speaking. "Dad," he said softly.

Mrs. Reed darted her head in his direction. "Dad? What did Dad do? Besides leaving? I mean, he left all of us, not Kaya specifically."

"I don't know about that," Graham said. "I've been thinking a lot about what Kaya said Dad was thinking that day when he hugged her. She thought it was the first voice she ever heard. She said that when she questioned him, he didn't ask her how she knew what he was thinking. He gave her a look like he was scared. He had been thinking that he wished he had control over it. What is 'it'? If I had heard all of this before, it wouldn't have made any sense. But now, with everything we know . . ." He paused. "Mom, is it possible that Dad's like Kaya?"

Mrs. Reed's eyes went wide. "Like Kaya?" she asked. "You mean, that he can hear people's thoughts? I—no, he couldn't. At least, I don't think so . . ." Her voice trailed off.

"He said he couldn't control it," Graham said. "What couldn't he control? And it seems like he suspected something was going on with Kaya, and he couldn't help her. I wonder if it's possible that that wasn't the first time Kaya read his thoughts. He was aware that something was happening to her. He was scared. He wanted to help her, but he couldn't."

A deafening silence filled the room for a long time. Then Mrs. Reed spoke. "He said he needed to get away," she said softly. "He needed to go where he could be alone, away from everyone. 'Off the grid' was how he put it."

Graham nodded. "He wanted to be somewhere that he wouldn't have to hear them anymore."

He touched his mother's hand. For a moment, he wondered if somehow he would be able to read her thoughts, but he couldn't.

"Kaya has the same abilities he had. It was too much for him. He had to get away. He couldn't watch her go through what he went through when it happened to him. He panicked. And once he left . . ."

"He couldn't come back," Mrs. Reed whispered. "Graham, I need some time with this. I need to think about this. I was with this man for twenty years. How could he have been going through something like this for so long, and have never told me?" Her face went pale. "What if he could read my thoughts? What did he hear? What was I thinking?"

Tears rose to her eyes.

"Graham, when he left . . . it was during a period of time when things were hard. Kaya had just turned fourteen. She wasn't the easiest child during that time. You were about to be a senior, and I was having a lot of worries about paying for a good college for you. There was a lot of turn-over at work, and so much more was being expected from me. I was very stressed. I had less time for him. What could I have been thinking back then? Could there have been a night when we were in bed, and he reached out for me, and I thought—I thought that I wanted him to leave me alone and give me space? I could see thinking something like that, but it would just be in the moment. Not that I would want him to go away and leave me alone forever."

She bent over, and although she wasn't shaking with sobs, Graham could tell she was lost in her tears. He looked up. Grayson was staring at them both in disbelief, and Gina had tears in her own eyes.

He reached over and put his arm around his mother.

"Mom," he said. "Mom. There's no way you could have known."

She looked up. "Maybe I should have," she said. "I loved him. I still love him. That will never go away. I should have known that something was going on. How can you love someone and not know? Kaya . . . and your father." Her head went back down. "I let them down," she whispered.

Graham pulled his mother into an embrace and held her tight.

"We let them both down," he said, circling his hand on her back. "But it's not our fault. It's no one's fault. This—this is beyond anything we could have known, or expected. We have to figure this out, Mom. You, and me, and Kaya."

"And me," Gina said, placing her hand on Graham's arm.

"And me," Grayson said, grasping Mrs. Reed's shoulder.

They sat that way for quite some time, until finally they all pulled away and composed themselves. Then Graham picked up the hotel phone and dialed Dr. Blake's number to make a plan for the next day.

CHAPTER 16

"THANK YOU FOR SEEING US on such short notice," Dr. Blake said as he shook Dr. Franklin's hand. Graham shook his hand as well, feeling like he needed to disinfect his skin immediately after. Instead, he sat in the chair offered and wiped his hand on his slacks.

"It's a pleasure to meet you, Dr. Franklin," Dr. Blake went on. "I've heard a lot about your hospital, and the care offered to the patients."

Graham noticed that Dr. Blake had neglected to say what it was he had heard about it.

Dr. Franklin smiled. "Thank you, Dr. Blake. As you must know, your reputation precedes you. I've been familiar with your work for years. As a matter of fact, I think you wrote the textbook for my undergrad Psych 101 class, many years ago."

Dr. Blake let out a jolly laugh. "Yes, I've been around since Hector was a pup." He looked at Graham. "It's an old saying, implying that I'm ancient." Turning back Dr. Franklin, he said, "I was sad to see that Miss Reed was admitted to the hospital after an incident. I don't know if you were aware that I had been working with her for the last two months."

Dr. Franklin's forehead creased. "In what capacity?" he asked. "I was not aware that you did clinical work, Doctor."

Dr. Blake shook his head. "That's because I don't. You see, Mr. Graham—"

Graham leaned in closer. "It's Mr. Reed, Professor. First name Graham."

Dr. Blake nodded. "Oh, yes," he said. "I was just testing to see whether or not you were paying attention. Mr. Reed is in my program at the university, and has been in several of my classes. Three years ago, he came to me to talk about his sister and her unusual symptoms. That led to several more conversations, and a rather unconventional collaboration. I met Miss Graham—I mean, Miss Reed—last year when she came to visit, and she agreed to participate in some research with me. You see, I was intrigued by her condition. She had been hearing voices for three years, with no sign of disability. She was able to function in her life like a normal teenager, participating in cheerleading, having a boyfriend, and getting decent grades in school. She showed no other symptoms, and the presentation of her auditory hallucinations was quite different from any other subject I'd ever studied."

"How so?" Dr. Franklin said, folding his hands in front of him on his desk. Graham was coming to realize that this was a sign that someone had his attention.

"Miss Reed's hallucinations are exclusively of the voice of the person standing beside or in front of her. At least in proximity to her location. The messages she receives present themselves as thoughts coming directly from the person. As if they were speaking their thoughts to her. Have you ever seen anything like that, Doctor?"

Dr. Franklin shook his head. "I have not," he admitted. "But auditory hallucinations often present themselves differently to each individual experiencing them."

Dr. Blake nodded. "Indeed," he said. "But something else caught my attention. Well, actually two things. The first is that the content was so benign. So benign as to include thinking she heard one classmate say that he had a sesame seed stuck between his teeth, and he needed some floss. Very mundane, actually. Sometimes, she could hear humming, or singing. Other times, it appeared that a young man might be having romantic thoughts about one of her friends. Very unusual indeed."

"And the other thing?" Dr. Franklin asked.

"Excuse me?" Dr. Blake asked.

Dr. Franklin looked slightly impatient. "You said there were two things that caught your attention. What was the second thing?"

"Ah, yes," Dr. Blake said, sitting back in his seat. "It's nice to see you're paying attention. Yes. The second thing is that Miss. Reed appears to be extremely perceptive."

"How do you mean?" Dr. Franklin asked. Graham thought he might have picked up on the slightest bit of nervousness on the part of the hospital administrator.

Dr. Blake shrugged. "Miss Reed does a remarkable job interpreting expression and body language," he explained. "I've done some testing on her in my lab. She scored remarkably high in the area of perception. I suspect that this talent has led to the content of the voices she hears. Miss Reed is sometimes very much on the mark when it comes to her voices."

Dr. Franklin laughed. "Are you trying to tell me that the things she hears, or appears to hear, have a basis in reality?"

Dr. Blake nodded and pointed directly at the other man. "That's exactly what I'm saying, Dr. Franklin," he said. "Sometimes, Kaya's voices turn out to be quite near the truth."

Dr. Franklin pushed his chair back. "Dr. Blake," he said. "With all due respect, you are a very well-perceived member of our community, and I have learned a great deal from reading your work. But what you're saying right now, I can't see how any of it can stand up to any empirical study. The young lady in question clearly has a psychotic disorder, and it sounds like you've been putting ideas in her mind that the things she hears might be based on reality. Clinically, this sounds like a very dangerous direction to be taking."

Dr. Blake raised his eyebrows. "I can understand your skepticism, Dr. Franklin," he said diplomatically. "This is all new to me, as well, and I had to spend a lot of time reviewing my data and trying to reconcile it with my previous research."

Dr. Franklin shook his head. "To put this in another way, Dr. Blake," he said, "it appears that you are saying that Miss Reed can read the thoughts of people around her."

Graham looked up. "I didn't hear Dr. Blake say that," he said. "He said that she can perceive the thoughts of the people around her, and then she translates those impulses into auditory hallucinations. Isn't that correct, Doctor?"

Graham saw Dr. Franklin shoot him an annoyed look. He had not made friends with the good doctor in the past few days.

"That is correct, Reed," he said. "I have not made any mention of anything supernatural, Doctor. I have just said that I, as well as Kaya's family, have noticed that she has an amazing accuracy when she conjectures as to what other people are thinking. You, for example, Dr. Franklin."

Dr. Franklin was looking at something on his desk, but now he looked up at Dr. Blake. "Me?" he asked. "Just what exactly did she think she heard me thinking about?"

Graham spoke up. "The same thing she told you the other day," he said. "You told us that she was accusing you of some sort of financial fraud with insurance. She told us the same thing."

Dr. Franklin's face grew dark, but Graham could tell he was getting worried about where this conversation was going. "The rambling of a psychotic girl," he said, picking up his pen. This was the same action he had taken a few days earlier right before dismissing Graham and his mother. "A homicidal girl who has been suffering from mental illness for many years, and had a recent break, causing more severe symptoms. You think that what she was saying about me was based in truth? Gentlemen, I am seriously considering ending this conversation right now. This is absurd! I feel like someone might break out a crystal ball any moment and tell me they can see my future. I don't want to entertain this type of talk any longer." He stood up.

"Are you still keeping your ledger locked in the file cabinet in the basement?" Graham said calmly, still sitting in his chair, his legs crossed in front of him.

Dr. Franklin stopped and turned sharply to face Graham. "Excuse me? What are you talking about?"

Graham shrugged. "Your ledger. The blue one. The one that you use to keep track of the actual services you're providing. You know, before you 'cook the books.'"

Dr. Franklin sat back down and glared at Graham. "I have no idea what you're going on about, young man, but I'm warning you. Don't you dare make accusations that you can't back up."

"Or what?" Graham asked. "You're gonna put me on a hold and bring me to a commitment hearing?"

Dr. Franklin was getting angry. Graham could see his face turning red. "What is it you're trying to get at, Mr. Reed?"

"It's just that I was under the impression that Medicare fraud was illegal," he said. "I have no idea how someone could get away with it for fifteen years, but I guess some people do. They have to really know what they're doing, and maybe even be in on it with another administrator at their establishment. Maybe someone who trusts them, but maybe wouldn't trust them as much if they found out that their partner was double crossing them."

A vein on Dr. Franklin's forehead started to pulsate. He stared at Graham and then at Dr. Blake. "What is it you want from me?" he asked quietly.

"Did Miss Reed make threats to go after the young man, Mr. Stratton?" Dr. Blake asked. "The one that she said was dangerous? Did she make threats against his life?"

Dr. Franklin closed his eyes for a moment. "No," he said, the sound of resignation in his voice.

"Does my sister really have symptoms of increased psychosis, such as paranoid delusions, Dr. Franklin?" Graham asked.

Dr. Franklin stared daggers into Graham's eyes. "She does not."

Dr. Blake nodded. "As I thought," he said lightly. "I'm usually correct in these situations. I've been doing this for some time, you know, Doctor."

He stood, motioning for Graham to stand, as well.

"I'll be going to Miss Reed's room to help her get her belongings together while you complete the paperwork to drop her hold and complete the discharge papers. Let's go, Graham."

"Wait!" Dr. Franklin said, getting to his feet again. "About the things you said, the details that you knew. How . . . ?"

Dr. Blake turned around and looked at Dr. Franklin. "I guess I have no idea what you're getting at, Dr. Franklin," he said. "We were just making conjectures. Whatever you heard us say, I cannot know. We will be waiting for you to give the discharge orders."

He left the office, Graham behind him, and walked straight for Kaya's room.

When they got there, Kaya was waiting anxiously. "Well?" she asked. "How did it go? Did it work?"

Dr. Blake fell onto Kaya's bed and wiped his brow. "Gather your things, Miss Reed," he said. "I imagine you'll be out of here within the next fifteen minutes. And I can pretty much guarantee that you'll never step foot in this hospital again in your life."

Kaya ran into her mother's arms. "I'm so sorry to have put you through this, Mom," she said through her tears. "It must have been so awful for you!"

Mrs. Reed pulled away, still holding her daughter's arms. "For me!" she exclaimed. "Kaya, I was only thinking about you, locked in that place, being forced to take medication that you didn't need."

She dropped her hands and took a step back.

"Kaya, all that time that I made you see the doctors, and tried to force you to take the pills—"

Kaya shook her head. "Mom, there's no way you could have ever imagined what was really going on with me. I mean, how could you? I don't even believe it, and it's me it's happening to! I'm still not really sure that it's real. It doesn't make any sense. How can I even do any of this? How can I read people's thoughts when I touch them? It's not possible. I've always wanted to believe there was such a thing as magic when I was younger, like fairies and stuff. But this is beyond that. This is me, not some movie. How do we even wrap our heads around this?"

She sat on the hotel bed.

Mrs. Reed shook her head. "I guess we keep working with Dr. Blake and try to learn as much as we can, and we just get used to the fact that there are things about our brains that we just don't understand. Kaya, maybe there is a scientific explanation. Maybe there isn't any magic to it."

She sat next to Kaya on the bed.

"Remember when you had your MRI back in high school, and the doctor said you had a strange, well, knoblike thing on the receptive language area of your brain?"

Kaya nodded. "The temporal lobe," she remembered. "He said it was probably a throwback to our caveman ancestors, kind of like the appendix."

"Right," Mrs. Reed said. "But what if it's something else? What if that little anomaly is what makes you hear thoughts?" She looked up at Dr. Blake.

Dr. Blake thought for a moment and then nodded. "Like your mother said, Miss Graham, there's a lot we don't know about the brain. There are millions, billions of human brains walking around the world every day, and there's no way we can take a good look at all of them. I would guess that there are many other anomalies out there that we'll never see. There might be an endless number of differences that we never find out about."

Graham smiled. "Can you imagine that, Kaya?" he asked. "It's that band of superheroes we used to talk about. Maybe they *are* out there, just waiting for you to find them. Maybe it's like all of those movies about mutants with special powers. Could you imagine what it would be like if you all banded together?"

Kaya laughed. "The Enigma and her Band of Merry Misfits!"

Everyone else laughed, and then there was a knock on the door. Assuming who it would be, Kaya ran to the door and threw it open, throwing herself into Grayson's arms.

"I've missed you so much," she said softly. She held him tight, and then pulled away. "I love you, too, and yes, I promise you don't have to worry about me ever going away like that again. Okay?"

Grayson smiled and nodded. Then he embraced Kaya again.

Graham smiled, too. He figured that Grayson would never have to say another word to Kaya again if he chose not to. She would always know what he was thinking. If he had anything to hide, he would have to keep his distance from her touch.

Ten minutes later, Gina arrived, and Dr. Blake offered to take them all out to dinner, Kaya's choice.

"I want a huge juicy steak," she said, and then she grinned. "Mashed potatoes. Squash. And a huge hunk of chocolate cake for dessert."

Dr. Blake nodded. "I know just the place."

They sat around the table, talking, making jokes, and just enjoying being in each other's company.

"So Kaya," Gina said after swallowing a bite of seared salmon, "I guess you won't be taking a leave of absence then."

Kaya shook her head. "No reason to," she said. "There's nothing wrong with me. The semester's about halfway over now, and I can get through it. I'll take some time to relax and think about things during Thanksgiving and winter break. I only missed a few days of school." She turned to Dr. Blake. "Can you help me if any of my professors give me a hard time?"

Dr. Blake nodded. "Of course, Miss Graham," he said. "I'd be happy to. They have to provide accommodations for students with medical issues, so you shouldn't have any problem. And you don't have to give them any specific information about what your medical condition was."

"Thank you so much," Mrs. Reed said. "And by the way, Dr. Blake, my daughter's name is Miss Reed, not Miss Graham. My son's first name is Graham."

Graham laughed. "Mom, don't worry about it. I have the feeling that Dr. Blake is quite aware of my name. I think this whole absentminded professor thing is just his persona, right, Professor?"

Dr. Blake looked at him, confused. "Persona? Like what, another personality? No, Reed, I honestly have no idea what you're going on about."

He sliced off a piece of his chicken breast, put it in his mouth to chew, and then turned to ask Grayson what he wanted to major in.

Graham looked at his sister, who was watching the interaction, looking amused. She appeared to feel his gaze upon her, and she turned to face him. She smiled. Graham smiled back. They continued to look at each other for some time, and then Kaya nodded at her brother. He nodded back. Kaya turned her attention back to Dr. Blake and Grayson, and she joined their conversation. Graham turned to Gina and his mother, and they talked about what costume the couple would be wearing for Halloween if they decided to go to a party. Gina suggested they dress as Jack Sparrow and Elizabeth from *Pirates of the Caribbean*, and how it would be a nice contrast to Kaya and Grayson's SpongeBob and Patrick. Graham laughed. He was feeling happy. It was a good feeling. He was hoping it was a feeling he could hold on to for a long, long time.

$\mathcal{C}$HAPTER 17

"I'VE BEEN THINKING ABOUT STUDYING law enforcement," Kaya said.

Graham's eyebrows shot up. "Really? I've never heard you talk about that before. What brought that on?'

Kaya leaned against the wall and then let herself slide onto the floor into a seated position. She patted the floor beside her, and Graham sat down, too. "It was my talk with Sergeant Morris last month. I've met with him a few times to talk about the Ted Stratton situation, and he said he thought that I had a good mind for police work."

Graham laughed. "Good mind indeed," he said. "You could solve all of his cases for him! Although I'm not sure that there are that many cold cases in a college police department."

"You'd be surprised," Kaya said. She reached into her purse, extracted her cell phone, and sent a quick message. Then she pulled out a pack of gum and took a piece. She held it out to Graham, and he took one too. "Did you know that the college police department has jurisdiction over any case that happens on campus? So if two people are walking through campus, even if they don't go to school there, and one kills the other one, the campus police get the case. They don't turn things over to the city police."

"Huh," Graham said as he pushed his gum into his mouth. "I had no idea. I didn't even know they were real cops."

Kaya nodded. "Some cops take jobs there kind of as a retirement job, since it really isn't as harsh as working in a city department, but sometimes, they do get pretty bad cases. Sergeant Morris says that the Ted Stratton case is one of them. I told you about the complaints they had gotten about him even before my incident with him, but there was never enough evidence to investigate or arrest him. I told him I would do whatever I could to help. He was thankful, but I don't think he one hundred percent believes in my ability to hear thoughts. I offered to prove it to him, but he kinda pulled his hands away. Maybe he'll let me try someday. At least he doesn't think I'm crazy anymore. Just eccentric."

She looked at her watch.

"Do you think he forgot about us? He's ten minutes late. I mean, the guy is like ninety-eight years old."

Graham laughed. "Kaya, Dr. Blake is about sixty-five years old. Not even. He's not really that ancient. One of his students probably stopped him after class to ask a question. I used to do that all the time."

Kaya shrugged. "It's okay," she said. "I'm just excited to hear what he has to tell me. I've waited a long time. I wish Mom could be here to hear it, too."

"We'll call her from my place tonight," Graham promised. "I still can't believe she's still dating Dr. Flagg. He's the first guy she went out with. I never really liked that guy as a dentist. I just associate him with painful needles and a numb tongue."

Kaya laughed. "Numb tongue. I could make so many jokes right now about him and Mom and a numb tongue, but you'd probably not appreciate them."

"There's Dr. Blake," Graham said, getting to his feet and offering Kaya his hand. He sent her a quick message.

"Don't worry," Kaya said. "I'll be respectful. I only make the age jokes to you."

"Hello, Graham siblings," Dr. Blake said as he rushed to the door and unlocked it. "Come in. Sorry to be late. I couldn't find my blazer. It turns out it was on the back of a chair, under my winter jacket. I should have thought to look there first."

He turned on the lamp on his desk and motioned for his guests to sit down.

"I know you're anxious to see your results, Kaya, so let's get right to it."

He removed a file from his attaché case and pulled out some papers. He pushed aside several piles of student essays and laid the documents down.

"I have the written report, but I thought I'd let you read that on your own. What I wanted to show you was the images from the fMRI session we had last week."

He grabbed a paper from the stack and turned it around so Kaya and Graham could easily read it.

"So Kaya, I told you that we would be focusing on the areas of your brain that deal with receptive language. We took several images with you listening to regular speech, then some with no auditory stimuli at all, and then, with you holding on to either my hands or Graham's hands as we attempted to send you messages. We did some when we just held hands passively. And lastly, we did all of those images again using subjects you had never met before to see if there was a different result."

"Was there?" Kaya asked, sitting on the edge of her seat.

"As far as the strangers versus people you know, there was no difference at all. But I'd like you to look at the difference between the images of you listening to spoken language as opposed to the voices you heard through thoughts."

Graham and Kaya leaned closer to get a better look. "That one area is all lit up in red," Kaya said, pointing. "It's lit up in this one too, but this one also has a bit that's lit up on the left that's not on the first image."

Dr. Blake nodded. "Exactly," he said. "I'm not going to use too much fancy scientist language with you, although I had a mighty fine time doing that with my colleague when I first saw the pictures. Don't worry, I did not reveal whose brain this was, or what I was looking for, so your secret's still safe. But here's what we're looking at in the first picture. It's the left superior temporal gyrus, transverse temporal gyri, or Heschl's gyri and the left temporal lobe. This part lights up with auditory stimulus. So Kaya, when you hear speaking, it lights up like normal. In the second image, as you can see, it also lights up when your brain is taking input from reading thoughts."

"Oh my God," Graham said softly. "So her brain actually shows that she's hearing something."

"Yes," Dr. Blake said. "It's the same result we expect to see from subjects who experience auditory hallucinations. Basically stimuli that's coming from the brain, not through the nerves in the ears. But the most fascinating finding is that little bit that you saw to the left, Kaya."

"What is it?" she asked.

Dr. Blake shrugged. "I have no idea. I'm not afraid to tell you that I'm stumped, and so was my colleague. What I think it is, is that anomaly that your doctor saw four years ago in your MRI. The one he thought might be a genetic throwback. And you know, I suspect that he might be correct."

"So what does it do?" Graham asked, his eyes still scanning all of the images, taking them in.

"I'm not sure," Dr. Blake said. "The voices were predictable, as we can see from the images, but the part that we don't understand is how they travel from the person's head, through touch, into Kaya's nervous system to be interpreted. My suspicion is that the little knob there, the one that lit up, is what causes that to happen."

"But why would our ancestors have something like this?" Kaya asked, looking up from the images at Dr. Blake. "It seems like it might be a kind of advanced thing, like something that would come from evolution rather than a throwback."

Dr. Blake shook his head. "I don't think so," he said. "This is what I think: I think that hundreds of thousands of years ago, the first humans didn't have language like we know it now. They didn't have an oral way to communicate. Yet, they seemed to be able to collaborate to survive. What if they did communicate? What if they were able to 'hear' each other's thoughts? Now, I don't mean in the exact way you do, Kaya. More like images. Say they were hunting the saber-toothed tiger. One of the hunters sees the tiger, but the other has his back to it. See, I'm not sure that they had to use touch like you do, Kaya. So the one who sees the tiger sends a silent warning to the other hunter, who spins around and hits the tiger on the head with a rock. Okay, well, that's kind of a simplistic explanation, but it's a start. Or maybe they did rely on touch, too. Maybe that was how couples worked out their sex lives. They obviously had sex, as the species continued. I'd imagine that your talent would be a pretty spectacular skill to have in the bedroom—"

"Okay," Graham said. "So our caveman fathers might have had this same part of the brain." He tried to wipe the thoughts of Kaya and Grayson in the bedroom out of his mind. "And I guess over the years, when they learned to communicate verbally, they didn't need to use that part anymore, and it got weaker, and over the centuries, it just faded away. But now here it is in Kaya's brain. I wonder why, out of all people, Kaya has that little knob. And maybe my father. So do you think that means that going back generations, a lot of our direct ancestors had the same thing?"

Dr. Blake nodded. "I do. I don't know if it expressed itself the way Kaya's does, or for that matter, your father's. It's possible that something activated it. Maybe all the technology we have today. All of the electronics. The headphones. The loud rock and roll. Cellular phones. Cellular phones would be my guess, since the sound waves move through air. Many people suspect that they cause a negative impact, but that's unsubstantiated."

Kaya stared at the floor. "So I guess this means that we have a general idea of how this all happens, scientifically." She shook her head. "So it's not magic. I guess I'm relieved, and disappointed at the same time. But it makes me wonder what other parts of the brain have been used and discarded through the years, and if anyone else has my skill, or other skills that we no longer need to survive. I think a lot of people would still see it all as magic, even if there is a scientific explanation. A lot of people don't believe science. I don't understand that. The proof is right there in front of their eyes. But it could be dangerous if someone is suspected of practicing magic, like back in the days of witch trials. So if anyone else has any skills like mine, they would most likely keep them quiet, don't you guys think?"

Graham nodded. "Yeah," he said. "I bet they do. I would be so curious to know what else is out there, what else people can do. But Kaya, I'd be worried about people finding out about you, too, for other reasons. I could see some people wanting to use your skill for really bad reasons, like for spying, or committing crimes."

"I agree with both of you," Dr. Blake said. "That's why I've decided that I'm not taking this research any further."

Kaya blinked. "I'm not sure how I feel about that," she said. "Dr. Blake, this is huge. No one has ever researched any of this—"

"That we know of," Dr. Blake clarified.

Kaya sat back. "Oh, that's true. I didn't think of that. But if you did pursue it, it could really make the end of your professional career really spectacular. I know that you told Graham that you've always wanted to discover something new in mental health, and there hasn't really been anything new since the invention of the atypical antipsychotics. I'd hate to see you lose this opportunity."

Dr. Blake smiled at her. "Kaya, I'm not missing out on anything," he said gently. "I'm experiencing exactly what I'd hoped to experience. You see, it's not only about publishing and sharing this knowledge with the world. It's about knowing it's there, and that there's more out there to be discovered, and we haven't even come close to discovering all of what's out there. Can't you see what an amazing thing that is? Kaya, that's enough for me. Maybe someday Reed will be the one to write this paper. He'll have more information, and be able to present enough to the world so that they'll know that it is science and not magic, and we can head in new directions. I'm happy to leave that legacy to Reed."

Graham beamed. "Thank you, Dr. Blake," he said. "But Reed is my last name. First name Graham."

Dr. Blake nodded. "You really should get something done about that, Reed."

"Well, that was pretty awesome," Kaya said as they left Dr. Blake's office half an hour later. He had reviewed more images with them and answered several questions. After those questions, Dr. Blake came up with a dozen more to explore. "I'm really glad Dr. Blake agreed to continue to do some research with me, even if he doesn't publish the results. I'm especially excited about him doing the fMRI on you, Graham, to see if you have that knob. You know, we should name the knob. Knob sounds so . . . I don't know . . . phallic?"

Graham laughed. "It really does," he said. "And I really don't want to hear Dr. Blake talk about the sexual advantages of your knob anymore!" He shook his head. "I might need to wash out my brain with soap now."

Kaya smiled. "Let's go get some something hot to drink while we're out," she suggested. "You don't have any more classes today either, right?"

Graham shook his head. "Should we go to Edward's coffee cart so you can have some eye candy with your cocoa?"

Kaya blushed. "It's not candy if you don't eat it."

They entered the large building and stood in line for their drinks.

"I'm glad I know what causes my, you know, *talent,*" Kaya said, whispering the last word so others in line couldn't hear. "I can relax now, and move on. It's so great that science can explain everything, isn't it?"

"It is," Graham said, taking a step forward as the line moved quickly. "That's why research is so interesting. I like the idea that Gina came up with, about taking a year to work as a research assistant, to figure out if I want to go further in the field later. I brought it up to Dr. Blake last month, and he said that he could put the word out in the department to see if anyone's interested. I'll have to come up with some other ideas, too, in case that doesn't work out, but that would be ideal. I have to come up with some way to make money before Gina and I get married."

He ordered his drink, and then stood aside so Kaya could order hers.

"It's on me," he told his sister as he handed his debit card to Edward.

Kaya smiled. "Thanks."

They brought their drinks to an empty table and sat down.

Graham took off his coat and hung it on the back of his chair. He watched Kaya unwrap her scarf and remove her hat. "I can't believe it's only about five months until I graduate," he said. "I remember the first time I came in here freshman year. It all looked so huge."

Kaya took a sip of her drink. "Remember when you brought me here that time, to see the empty lecture hall? Yeah, I was a bit overwhelmed that day. I remember thinking that there would be no way I could concentrate in there, with all the chaos, and all the people. But now I know what causes it, and I can control it better. It's gotten so much easier. In a way, that trip to the psychiatric hospital helped all of us figure it all out."

"Yeah," Graham agreed. He laughed. "It might not have been that long ago, but I'll never forget that day when I saw the news and they were leading Dr. Franklin out of Benson Hospital in handcuffs. Tax evasion and Medicare fraud. Hundreds of thousands of dollars stolen from the federal government. And I still wonder who called the tip in to the authorities."

"I always assumed it was Dr. Blake," Kaya said, dabbing at her lips with her napkin.

Graham shook his head. "He swears it wasn't him," he said. "I would imagine a guy like that makes a lot of enemies in his lifetime. I just want to know who it was so I could thank him. What he did to you was unforgivable. I wonder how many lives he ruined, just to be able to pad his own bank account."

"I wonder how many other people like me have passed through the mental health system," Kaya said. "It's sad enough to have to deal with mental illness, but having to be subjected to mental health medications and treatment when you're not really mentally ill is so tragic."

"It really is," Graham said. He drank the last few sips of his tea. "Do you want to head back to my place?"

"I'm not quite done," Kaya said, looking down at her drink. Then she looked up. "Oh, there's a girl from my English class over there. Her name's Priya. She's really nice."

The girl started to walk toward them. Another girl trailed behind her.

"She's coming over here. Quick. Wipe your mouth. You have something on your lip."

Priya approached the table with a smile. "Hi, Kaya. It's nice to see you again. This is my sister, Jade."

Kaya smiled warmly. "Nice to meet you, Jade. This is my brother, Graham. Do you want to join us? We're heading out soon, but we're not in a huge hurry."

Priya turned to Jade, and a look passed between them. Jade nodded, and the two women sat down. "I'm glad we ran into you, Kaya. I haven't seen you since last term. I never got to talk to you after you had your, um, accident?"

"I was there," Jade said quickly. "I was walking back to my apartment that night, and I was one of the people who stopped to try to help."

Kaya's lips parted for a moment in thought. "Oh," she said. "Well, I guess thank you.'

Jade reached out and put her hand over Kaya's. "Don't be embarrassed," she said. "I can tell you're worried about what I saw, but I understand. I wanted to share something with you. That's why I had Priya bring me over here."

Kaya looked down at Jade's hand and then at her eyes. Then she looked at Graham. Her shoulders relaxed.

"Okay. Thank you. Yes. You have something to tell me."

Jade nodded. "The reason I wanted to come over to talk to you was because you were right about that guy, Ted Stratton."

Graham's ears perked up. "You know him?"

"Indirectly," Jade said. "My friend, Becca, she knew him freshman year. He was part of her group of friends from our dorm."

"But something happened," Kaya said, encouraging Jade.

Jade nodded. "Something happened. Becca, well, she liked Ted. She had a crush on him, and he knew it. He flirted with her, and led her on. It almost seemed cruel the way he played with her like she was a kitten. She didn't want to listen to me when I told her it seemed weird. She thought it was a cultural thing for me, and said that she didn't mind the cat and mouse game. Then one day, he asked her out. She was ecstatic! She got all dressed up, and borrowed makeup and shoes from our floormates, and she was incredibly nervous. It was kind of cute, actually. I was happy for her, because it seemed like finally the game was over, and Ted was giving her what she wanted."

"Then what happened?" Graham said, fearing he already knew part of the answer.

"She didn't come home that night," Jade said softly.

"Oh, no," Kaya said, almost in a whisper.

Jade shook her head. "It was late morning, and her roommate, Cass, hadn't heard from her at all. She called the campus police, saying she was worried about her. They told her that there was nothing they could do. They said she probably went home with someone, and would be back soon. Cass didn't believe that. She thought that Becca would have been in touch by then. So she grabbed me and my roommate Tammy, and we went to Ted's room. We found him there alone, all showered and dressed. He greeted us with a smile, and told us he was surprised to see us. We told him that we couldn't find Becca, and he seemed really worried. He said he had left her off at the elevator on our floor, said good night, and then went back to his room to go to bed. He couldn't imagine what had happened to her. That's when we got really scared, and Cass called the police back to tell them. Then they took her seriously. They started a search. It was two hours later that they found her."

Kaya gasped. "Dead?"

"Almost," Jade said. "They found her unconscious in an alley behind a bar, behind a dumpster. She had been assaulted. The police didn't tell us how she'd been assaulted, but we knew. They took her to the hospital, where she was unresponsive for days. Finally, she started to wake up, and her parents were there. The police tried to question her, but she couldn't answer them. She cried. She was in pain, and I think she knew that something terrible happened, but just didn't remember the details. We were allowed to see her once she became more stable. She was a shell of a person. Her shine, her enthusiasm, all gone. So was the necklace she was wearing that night, one she had gotten from her parents for her high school graduation. She loved that necklace. After the doctors said she was stable enough to be moved, Becca's parents brought her back home to receive treatment there. She never came back to school. Nothing ever happened. No one knew who had attacked her, or why she had been there. She didn't remember what had happened. The campus police had to let it go."

"But you think it was Ted," Graham said.

Jade nodded. "I suspected, and so did her other friends," she said. "His story didn't make any sense. If he dropped her off at the elevator, how did she end up at the bar? She was out with the guy she really liked. She wouldn't have gotten home and then gone back out. She wasn't a drinker. Yeah, a beer or two, but not heavy. She wasn't with any friends, and we couldn't imagine anyone else luring her out. But the kicker came some months later."

"What was it?" Kaya said. She looked down at her cocoa. The rest of her drink had gone cold as she listened to the story. She pushed it away.

"I was at a party," Jade said, "and I was talking to a girl I knew from back home. Then her friend came over and started talking to us, too. After a few minutes, I noticed her necklace. It was very distinctive. It was a gold shell with a real pearl in the middle. It was just like Becca's necklace, the one that went missing the night she was assaulted. I told her that I liked it, and asked her where she got it. She told me that she found it in a box in her boyfriend's room, and she asked him about it, thinking he had bought a gift for another girl. He told her that it was a gift he had gotten for her, but he was waiting for her birthday to give it to her. But he gave it to her right then because she had found it."

Kaya grimaced and looked at Graham. He grabbed her hand and sent her a message. *Ask the question*, he said. Kaya nodded slightly.

"Her boyfriend was Ted Stratton," she said. "Right?"

Jade's eyes darkened. Then she nodded. "He had kept it. I would assume that if he hadn't been the one to assault her, then he would have given the necklace to her parents after it happened. Instead, it seemed like he had taken it as a trophy. A fucking trophy!" Jade turned to Priya. "Don't tell Mommy about my language please. But yes, from that day on, I was positive that Ted had been the one to attack Becca. I did go to the police to let them know, but again, I didn't have any proof of any of this, just conjecture. He could have bought a similar necklace at the store. But I know he didn't."

Graham nodded. "I know that that guy is bad news," he said. "The police know too. Kaya was not wrong to feel threatened by him that night. She's been back to talk to Sergeant Morris, to follow up. The police have their eye on him."

"They do," Kaya said. "Sergeant Morris said he'll make it his personal quest to make sure no girl ever gets hurt by that guy. He told me there were other reports given about him, and I'm guessing one of them came from you, Jade. There may be others."

"Sergeant Morris was the one I talked to," Jade said. "I could tell that if he could, he'd bring Ted in himself, and take care of him personally. He told me that his daughter was planning on coming to State the next year, and he wanted the campus to be safe not only for her, but for all women. I believed him."

Kaya touched Jade's hand again. After a moment, she spoke. "I can tell you feel some relief from telling me this, Jade," she said. "I'm glad. You really validated me by telling me about Becca. I'm just so sorry that all of that happened to your friend. You know, I knew, right away, that that boy was not right in the head. I've talked to Sergeant Morris about starting a walking escort service on campus for students so they don't need to walk home alone after sundown if they don't feel comfortable. If you'd like to get involved in getting that started, I can give you my number, and you can be part of it."

Jade smiled. "I'd like that very much, Kaya. It's something that I can do to honor Becca, to make her ordeal have some meaning. Because otherwise, it's just pure tragedy. Someday I hope to be able to tell her that I did something to make it better."

After Jade and Priya left, Graham and Kaya threw away their trash and headed back to Graham and Gina's apartment.

"I think I'll have Grayson come over to walk me home later," Kaya said. "You know, just because."

Graham nodded. "If he can't, Gina and I will walk you home. Or drive you."

Kaya sighed as she walked. "I feel better and worse knowing Becca's story," she said. "Like I told Jade, I feel validated, but there was this hope in me that Ted hadn't acted on his horrible thoughts yet. I guess that was pretty naive of me."

"There's nothing wrong with optimism," Graham said.

Kaya reached out and took his hand as they walked. Graham knew it made her feel safer to know she could read his thoughts. "Why are you thinking about him?"

"About Ted?" Graham wondered.

Kaya shook her head. "No. Dad. You're thinking about Dad. You're wondering about him. He suddenly popped into your head. Nothing really succinct."

Graham shrugged and then thought about it. "Something about optimism." He squeezed Kaya's hand.

She nodded. "Optimism," she said. "It was from a long time ago. We were talking about Dad, and I told you that I thought he would be there to walk me down the aisle when I got married. I was pretty sure. You complimented my optimism. Maybe that's it."

Graham stopped and looked at her. "Did I think all that?"

Kaya shook her head. "Sort of," she said. "It was sort of just there, inside of you, jumbled. I kind of pulled it together. Do you remember that conversation? I can kind of remember it."

Graham grinned. "That was much easier than using hypnotism to retrieve memories. I do kind of remember that. I guess that words can trigger thoughts and feelings. Do you still feel that way about Dad?"

"I don't know," Kaya said. "I guess I thought that he'd be back by now. It will be five years this spring. Every year that goes by, the more I believe that he's gone. I mean, I'm not sure if he's dead, or just gone. But gone. But there is that small piece of me that thinks he's still out there somewhere, and he'll make his way back to us. I haven't decided what that would be like for me. I want to feel angry at him for choosing to leave us at the time he left, and then every day since then that he's decided to not come back. But then, I also want to talk to him, to find out what made him leave. Did he understand what was going on with him? Did he ever talk to anyone about it? Did he think he was crazy, and by extension that I was going crazy, too? So in that way, I feel sorry for him. If he had come clean, maybe we would have been able to help each other. But I do want to tell you a secret, Graham."

"What is it?" Graham asked, his curiosity growing.

She leaned closer. "I know that someday Grayson and I are going to get married. I can feel it, and I can hear it in his thoughts. He wants that, and I want it too. So someday, Grayson and I will have a wedding. And when we do, I will most likely spend much of the day looking around, to the sides and behind me, to see if there is a strange man in the wings, watching, maybe with a tear in his eye. And once I see him, I will smile. I won't get mad. I will be happy. It'll be the happiest day of my life. And if he dares to come forward to greet me, I'll embrace him. And if after that he wants to be in my life, I'll let him. And if he doesn't want to be, I'll let him go. But I'll know then. I'll know he never forgot me. I'll hold him close, and I'll know everything there is to know about him, and he'll know everything there is to know about me. And you know what? That will be enough."

Acknowledgments

There are so many people to thank, so I'd like to start with the people who have been faithfully reading my McKinney High Class of 1986 series. Whenever I get a note from someone who tells me they enjoyed my books, and look forward to the next one, I get teary-eyed. It's what keeps me writing every day! And it's what inspired me to try to write paranormal fiction, a new genre for me. Thank you to my readers!

Also thank you to Jai Design for all of the hard work you have done for me on my covers and marketing my books, Nicole Frail for making me look good with my grammar and spelling, and Milana Gilligan for taking one of the best pictures I've ever had of myself! I will use it for every book, ever!

Thank you to my friends, in Portland, Massachusetts, and elsewhere who have believed in me, and to my family, who had been with me through it all. Thanks to Clint Chico, master author, and Jonathan Meltzer, for never hesitating to read my drafts.

And thank you Al and Tory. For everything ever.

About the Author

Debby Meltzer Quick is a full-time social worker in Portland, Oregon. She has been writing for fun since age twelve. Growing up in Massachusetts, she became a huge fan of Boston sports, especially the Red Sox and the Patriots, and she aspired to be a sports reporter. She is an avid reader of fiction. She lives with her husband, daughter, two cats, and one rabbit. She has completed two series of seven books each that take place in the fictional city of Eastboro, Massachusetts, in the 1980s. Watch for more books in the Anomaly series coming soon!

CHAPTER 1

PETER STOOD BEHIND THE HEDGE surrounding the courtyard to watch the ceremony. He knew he wouldn't be welcome by the family. His family. What used to be his family. But it had been his choice to walk away all those years ago.

He had never walked away completely. He had been watching them from afar for years.

Not in the ways of a stalker. The world had been invaded by the internet. Information could be found online. He saw when his daughter made the cheerleading team in high school and then when she was voted team captain during her senior year. He had found the yearly honor roll from his son's school every year on the digital version of the town's newspaper, and the list of names of the graduates when he finished school. His daughter was three years behind her brother, and then they were both at State University.

Lucky for Peter, who was adept in the ways of modern technology, social media was becoming easier and easier to access. He was able to see pictures and stories on MySpace, and then Facebook. He could see his children's activities and thoughts, at least the ones they made public. When he finally decided to make contact, he would have to urge them to be more private with who could see their information. But for now, he was glad it was available for him so he could track their progress in life.

It was harder to track his wife. She was now his ex-wife, he knew. He could see her progress at work as she got promoted through the years, making great strides even after she was left to raise their two children on her own with no financial assistance except the balance of their joint savings account. But the news that hit him hardest had been the announcement in the *Wisteria Weekly News.*

Janice had gotten engaged. And the man she was engaged to was the dentist he used to bring his children to see when they were small. The man that provided the children with a new toothbrush every six months.

Maybe Janice liked the perks. Maybe Dr. Flagg polished her teeth for free. What hurt the most was thinking about what else of Janice's he was polishing.

He hadn't left because he'd stopped loving his wife. He left because he *did* love her and their kids. He hadn't felt like he'd had a choice. And he didn't really regret his choice. The children were doing great. Janice was happy. And today, on this beautiful spring day in Wisteria, his daughter was getting married.

He watched as his son walk down the aisle, escorting his mother to her seat in front, and then he went back to walk his grandmothers to their seats beside their husbands. The bridesmaids started their trek, and Peter shook his head in disbelief. His daughter's friends had all grown up so much. He felt as though no time had passed, but this was the proof that it had. As if to mock him, his left knee started to ache again. He shifted his position to take some weight off of it.

Soon, his son walked back down the aisle, this time on the arm of a woman he had never met, but he knew she was his daughter-in-law. They took their place at the altar. A tear rolled down Peter's face as he realized that his daughter-in-law was obviously very pregnant. He was going to be a grandfather soon. He had already missed so much.

The music stopped. Peter looked to the back of the aisle, and he saw his daughter. She was a vision of absolute beauty, an angel, with her chestnut hair wrapped around the back of her head, wavy tendrils framing her face, her fragile features, her beaming smile. He wasn't close enough to see them, but he remembered her shining blue eyes. She was radiant. She was holding on to the arm of an older man whose face he couldn't see. He braced himself to see the dentist walking his daughter down the aisle on her wedding day. It was a job that should have gone to Peter, and it would have, if only he'd made a different choice . . . but if he had made a different choice, this wedding might be happening.

The music started. The Wedding March. Everyone stood as the bride made her way toward her true love. Peter tried to get a good look at the face of the dentist, only to find . . . it wasn't the dentist at all. It was a man he had never seen before. He was a man of average height, with a deeply receded hairline. What was left on his head was a tufty gray fringe, and he wore a pair of lopsided, round spectacles that appeared to be sliding toward the tip of his bulbous nose. He was wearing a black tux that matched all of the other men in the wedding, but on this man, the suit looked frumpy, as if he had slept in it the night before.

The man stumbled slightly, and Peter's daughter caught his arm. They looked at each other and giggled before continuing their walk. When they made it to the altar, the groom stepped forward to meet them. His daughter kissed the older man on the cheek, took the groom's hand, and went the last few steps to stand in front of the justice of peace to be joined in holy matrimony. The ceremony progressed, and then came to its conclusion. The bride and groom kissed, everyone applauded, and the wedding party receded back up the aisle. Peter wiped the tears from his eyes. They were tears of joy, and tears of loss.

Peter Reed had lost years with his family. They were years he had spent searching, trying to find the truth about himself, and by extension, his family. He had done what he'd felt he had to, to protect them, and to be completely honest, to protect himself. It made sense that they had all moved on. They had to. He wanted that for them. They were not obligated to stay in stasis until he returned. He wasn't even sure he was ready to return. He only wanted to watch and maybe establish some sort of brief contact—

"Hey, you, what are you doing back there?"

Peter turned to look behind him. A man dressed in the formal clothing of catering staff was holding a sealed trash bag in each hand, apparently bringing them out to the dumpster nearby. "I . . . uh, I'm just—"

"I told the other guy that came by earlier that the family said we could leave any leftovers out on the south side of the venue after everyone leaves. But in the meantime, you need to clear out." He turned to leave, but then turned back quickly. "Oh, will you all be needing utensils? I can make sure we leave you some plastic forks and knives. And maybe some disposable napkins if you want."

"I don't—I guess—"

The man shook his head. "Listen," he said apologetically. "I understand. I've been through some hard times myself. It's hard to believe that our country has come to this, especially in a place like Wisteria. I'm sorry they don't let you guys stay in the shelter during the daytime hours. I can't imagine it's easy to have to wander around all day. At least there are some shady trees at the park. If it gets too hot, I think the community center has an air-conditioned area where you can go and rest and get something cold to drink. And then come back later for the food. Probably around six?"

Peter stared at the man, and then he nodded. "Okay," he said. "Yeah, thank you. You've been very generous. I'll—I'll just go."

He turned back toward the courtyard and took one more look. He saw her, his daughter. Kaya. She was standing on the lawn, talking to the dentist. The dentist had his hand on her elbow. On her right was the groom. His name was Grayson Pike. His son-in-law. Peter swallowed. He took one more sweeping look over the group of guests at the reception. There was Janice, his ex-wife, talking to Peter's own parents, Tom and Candice. They all laughed. It made him happy to see them still being friendly with each other. Janice had never done anything wrong. She deserved to have their love and support. Maybe they had even befriended the dentist.

And there, sitting at another table, was Graham, his first-born child. Graham had become a man. He was sitting next to his wife. Her name was Gina. She had her hand on her protruding belly, and she was smiling. The older man, the one who had walked his daughter down the aisle, was sitting at the same table, and he was talking. He was also looking around, as if he had lost something. Then he bent down and looked under the table. He came back up and shrugged. Graham and Gina laughed.

Peter turned away. He was intruding here. He had to leave. If he didn't leave now . . . He took a few steps forward.

"Hey!"

Peter stopped, but he didn't turn around.

"Hey! You! Stop!"

Peter took another step toward the street, praying his face had been shielded well enough by his baseball cap.

"I said stop! Come on! I can't run in these heels. Give me a break."

Peter took a breath and closed his eyes. Then he opened them again and turned around. And there she stood, about twenty feet away. He took off his hat.

She ran up to the edge of the courtyard, looking over the hedge at the sidewalk. When he looked at her, she stopped in her tracks, her mouth agape, eyes focused on the sight before her. A full minute passed as they stared at each other. Just as she went to take a step toward him, her new husband was at her side.

"Kaya, what is it?" he asked, putting his hand on her arm.

She looked at him, and then back at Peter. She pointed. "Him."

"That's the guy I saw behind the bushes during the ceremony," Grayson said. "I'll go talk to him." He took a few steps toward the sidewalk, but Kaya grabbed his arm.

"Grayson," she said softly. "No." She held his arm tightly. "I . . . *I* need to go. Grayson, I thought he was just some creepy guy, gawking at us, but— that's—I think that's—"

"I'm her father," Peter said, taking a step toward her.

Kaya continued to stare, and then a sly smile spread across her face.

"I knew you'd come," she said. "I told Graham, years ago. I told him you'd come to my wedding, and you'd watch me get married, and then we'd talk . . ." She reached out toward him.

Peter quickly took a step back. "No, Kaya," he said. "No. Not yet."

Kaya jerked back, her arm still outstretched. She looked at her hand. "I . . . oh my God." She dropped her arm to her side. "So it's true," she whispered.

"What's true?" Grayson asked. He looked up and glared at Peter. "This is the absolute worst time that you could have shown up, Mr. Reed. This is our wedding day."

Kaya nodded slowly, looking at her feet. "It's the happiest day of my life."

Grayson looked at her. "Kaya, what do you want me to do?" he asked, desperate to do something. "How can I help you?"

Kaya looked at him gratefully. "Go get Graham, babe. But don't tell him why. Just tell him I need him right now."

Grayson nodded. He looked at Peter one more time, shooting him a warning look. "I'll be right back." He jogged away.

"He's great," Peter said. "I can tell. He really loves you."

Kaya laughed bitterly. "So you don't even need to touch him to tell, huh? I guess your skills are really advanced."

Peter smiled at his daughter, although confused by her words. "You don't need any special skills," he told her, "to be able to see when a man is madly in love with your daughter. I could see it in every part of him. You did great, Kaya."

"And you remember my name."

That statement ripped at Peter's heart. "Your name," he said. "I chose it, you know. Your mother had no idea what to name you. She was reading out loud from this baby name book she had taken out of the library. When she read off Kaya, I suddenly remembered a trip I had taken to Jamaica during spring break in college. These local guys were walking around the beach, trying to sell pot to tourists. They called it *kaya*. So when your mother said the name, it hit me funny, and I told her that was the name I wanted. I didn't tell her why at first. She just thought it was pretty."

"Everyone thinks it's pretty," Kaya said. "Some people ask me if it's Hawaiian. I looked it up. It actually is a Hawaiian word. It means 'the sea.' I think I like that better than meaning 'pot' in Jamaican."

Peter laughed. "Do you like the sea? Have you ever been?"

"No," she said, rubbing her arms with her hands, as if she were cold. "I plan to, though, someday."

Peter nodded. "We have so much to catch up on."

Grayson ran back over. "Graham is coming," he said. "He didn't want to leave Gina alone, so he was bringing her over to your mom." He turned to Peter. "She's almost full term."

Peter could tell that Grayson was trying to convey a message to him:

This is my territory. These are my people. You don't belong here. Watch your step.

Peter nodded. "I could see her earlier. She looks beautiful."

Kaya looked toward the courtyard as her brother walked calmly over to the small group.

"What's up, Ky?" he asked. "Are those homeless guys from before bothering you again?"

He looked toward the man on the sidewalk. At first, it appeared that he hadn't made the connection. Then he looked back again and nodded. "Hello, Dad," he said, still calm.

"Hello, Graham," he said. "Congratulations on the wife and baby."

Graham nodded. "Thank you," he said. He turned to Kaya. "Do you want me to . . . do anything right now?"

Kaya looked back and forth between her brother and her father. "He doesn't want me to touch him."

Graham thought for a moment. "So we were right then."

Peter watched his son's face. "What were you right about?" he asked quizzically.

"You have the skill," Graham said.

"What skill?" Peter asked.

"Oh for God's sake, Dad," Kaya exclaimed. "You know very well what skill."

"Maybe I do," Peter answered. "But maybe what some people call a skill, others call a curse."

"And that's why you left me to deal with the curse all by myself?" Kaya snapped.

Grayson stepped up. "I really don't think this is the right time to get into this." He turned to Graham for support.

Graham nodded. "Dad, I'm not sure what to do or say right now. Kaya suspected a long time ago that you would appear at her wedding, behind the bushes. You did exactly that. I also remember her telling me that when you did show up at her wedding, she wouldn't be angry, and she wouldn't turn you away." He looked at Kaya. "Remember that, Kaya? You said that you would listen to what he had to say."

Kaya's face softened. "I did say that."

"Kaya!" a female voice called out. "The photographer needs you."

Kaya looked back at Peter. "This is my wedding day," she said. "I-I guess I'm glad you showed up. It's like you fulfilled a prophecy. But like Grayson said, this is not the time or place to get into this conversation. I do want to talk to you. We have a lot to catch up on."

She reached for Grayson's hand.

"Wait!" Peter called out quickly. He didn't want the moment to end. He wanted to gaze at his daughter in her wedding dress for just a little bit longer. "Who was that guy, the one that walked you down the aisle? I know it wasn't Steve Flagg."

Graham shook his head. "You know about Steve?" he asked. "Well, I guess if you know about Kaya and Grayson getting married, you'd know about Mom and Steve's engagement."

"That's Dr. Blake," Kaya said. "He's a close family friend. Graham and I met him at State. He's . . . helped us a lot over the past few years. He's been, well, like a father to me. I couldn't think of anyone else I'd want to walk me down the aisle. And Dr. Blake, he knows things. About me. About us." She motioned to her brother. "And I guess, by association, about you, too."

Peter winced. "About me? What about me? What does this man know?"

Grayson spoke up. "Listen, Mr. Reed—"

"Peter, please."

Grayson nodded. "Peter. We have pictures to take, and people to greet. Graham, can you . . ."

Graham nodded. "You two go back. I'll be there in a few minutes."

Kaya gave Peter one last faint smile and then walked away with her husband, hand in hand.

Peter looked at Graham. There was so much he wanted to know, including what this Dr. Blake knew about his family, but right now, his son was standing right in front of him, all grown up. His face relaxed.

"You must be close to six feet tall."

Graham laughed awkwardly. "Five-ten. I think these shoes give me a little bit of extra height. I never got as tall as you, or even Grandpa." He looked more carefully at his father. "I guess it's a good thing for me that male pattern baldness comes from the mother's side of the family, huh?"

Peter's hand went straight to the top of his head. "It's not that. It's just some thinning on top. Most of it has grown back." He chuckled. "It started during a stressful period of time in my life, soon after I left . . . Wisteria. I started to pull some of it out methodically, when I was anxious. There's actually a name for it. Trichotrillomania."

"Huh," Graham said. "Is it hereditary?"

"I don't think so." Peter took a step onto the lawn, closer to his son. "Some things are just learned."

Graham nodded. "I'm in school to become a psychologist," he said. "I've been working in research for a few years, but now I'm back in grad school. It's a bit different than that path you took."

"To say the least," Peter said. "I guess advertising isn't for the faint of heart. But you've done well, Graham. I've followed your progress since high school."

Graham looked at the ground. "I always wondered if you knew what we were up to." He looked back up. "Internet?"

Peter nodded. "Internet. Son, I have to say I'm very proud of you. Of both you and Kaya. You've really done well. I was a bit skeptical when I saw that Kaya had been working for the police and was planning on attending the police academy. I'm both proud and scared for her. She's a brave girl."

"Woman," Graham corrected. "She's easily the bravest person I've ever known." He turned back to look at the crowd at the reception. He caught sight of Gina, still talking to his mother and her husband. "So do you want to wait, or do you want to talk about the elephant in the courtyard right now?"

Peter felt a palpitation in his chest. "The elephant?" he asked. "What elephant are you referring to?"

Graham smiled in amusement. "I might still be young, Dad," he said, "but I'm not stupid. It might have taken us a long time to figure out what was going on with Kaya, and most likely with you, but we did figure it out eventually, and the hard way. Dad, Dr. Blake has found out that Kaya has the anomaly. I've been tested, and I have it too, but it doesn't express itself the way Kaya's does. We're assuming we got the anomaly from your side of the family, but we'd have to do some testing to know for certain. We'd probably want to consider bringing in Grandma and Grandpa, too."

Peter looked at Graham, his eyes wide. "Son," he said, shaking his head. "You're gonna have to enlighten me. Because you're saying a lot of things here. A lot of confusing things. And to be honest with you, I have no idea what in the hell you're going on about."